THE SECRET PANEL

ANOTHER exciting mystery begins for Frank and Joe Hardy when they help a stranger who has had an accident with his car. The man introduces himself as John Mead, owner of a nearby estate. After he continues on his way, Frank finds an odd-looking house key which belongs to Mead. But when the Hardys try to return to it, they learn that John Mead died five years ago! They are even more amazed when they find that the intricately carved doors in the dead man's deserted mansion have no visible knobs or keylocks.

While working on this mystery, the boys assist their detective father in tracking down a highly organized ring of thieves who are robbing warehouses of television and stero equipment.

What happens when Frank and Joe discover that there is a link between Mr. Hardy's case and the mysterious Mead mansion will keep the reader on edge with thrills and suspense.

Behind the desk lay Chet Morton, bound and gagged!

Hardy Boys Mystery Stories

THE
SECRET
PANEL

BY

FRANKLIN W. DIXON

NEW YORK
GROSSET & DUNLAP
Publishers

CONTENTS

THE SECRET PANEL

CHAPTER I

A Startling Discovery

"STOP!"

Eighteen-year-old Frank Hardy jammed on the car brakes.

"What's the matter with that driver?" his brother Joe asked excitedly.

Racing down the hill toward them was a car evidently out of control. It zigzagged wildly from one side of the road to the other. Any moment it might crash head-on into the boys' convertible!

"Better back up!" Joe cried. "Look!"

The oncoming automobile swerved sharply, then dived into a ditch. At the same moment the left front wheel came off and rolled down the hill. Afraid that the wheel might bounce up on their open car, the boys scrambled out and jumped a fence to safety. The heavy wheel missed their convertible by inches and toppled over.

"Whew, that was a close one!" Frank remarked. "I wonder if the driver was hurt."

"We'd better find out," urged Joe, starting to run. He was blond and a year younger than his dark-haired brother.

When the Hardys reached the car, the driver, a lean man in his thirties, was still holding the steering wheel and seemed badly shaken.

"Are you all right?" Frank asked.

The stranger nodded slowly. "I think so. But I was never so scared in my whole life." He spoke with a British accent.

"I can imagine," Joe said.

"Shouldn't have let that boy in the garage change the tire," the man continued. "His boss was out and obviously he didn't know what he was doing. I might have been killed!"

Frank and Joe agreed. "Can we help you fix the car?" Frank asked.

"That'd be awfully decent of you. My name's John Mead."

The boys introduced themselves.

"The sons of the famous detective?" Mead asked, surprised. "I just read something in the paper about your father."

Joe nodded, then went to retrieve the wheel. Mead got out of the car and with Frank surveyed the lopsided automobile.

"I think we can get her back on the road," Frank observed. "Hey, Joe, give us a hand, will you?"

Together they righted the car, then Mead got a

jack and tools out of the trunk. Soon they had the wheel fastened again, and the Englishman started the engine.

"It's running fine," he said, relieved. "You chaps have been a great help. Thanks a lot. My home is on the north shore of Barmet Bay, a couple of miles from Bayport. Will you come and see me some time? I should be back in a week or so."

"We'll do that, sir," Frank replied with a grin. "Good luck!"

He and Joe pushed Mead's car out of the ditch, then the stranger drove off.

Joe stretched. "That's enough heavy work for one day," he said. "We're supposed to be on summer vacation!" Suddenly he stopped short. "Hey, Frank, take a look at this!"

"What is it?"

"A key. Sure looks funny."

Frank examined the large, strange-shaped object that Joe had picked up from the spot where the car had turned over.

"It must belong to Mead," he said. "Maybe we'd better take it over to his house later."

"He won't be there for a week, Frank."

"I know, but someone else might. Come on. Let's go."

On the way home they talked about the Englishman. "Did you notice the odd signet ring he was wearing?" Frank asked. "It reminded me of a square with three spokes."

"It did look strange," Joe commented.

When they arrived home they were greeted at the door by their father. Fenton Hardy was a tall, well-built man in his early forties. He had resigned from the New York Police Department years before, and attained fame as an expert detective when he went into private practice.

His sons were following in the elder Hardy's footsteps and in spite of their young age were excellent sleuths in their own right. Now, as they accompanied their father to his study, they sensed that something had gone wrong. Mr. Hardy frowned deeply as he sat down behind his desk.

Frank dropped into a soft upholstered chair. "What's the matter, Dad? You don't look too happy."

"New case, I bet," Joe put in.

"Right," Mr. Hardy said, looking at a typewritten sheet in his hand.

"Can you tell us about it?" Frank asked.

"Yes, I'm investigating a series of burglaries. Television and stereo equipment. Mostly stores and warehouses."

"Must be an organized gang," Frank observed.

"No doubt. What baffles me is the way they get in. All of the places have good burglar alarms, but they never go off. On the other hand, there is no evidence that the alarm systems were tampered with."

"Need help?" Frank offered.

"Not right now." Mr. Hardy grinned. "But I'll let you know if I do!"

Frank and Joe were always eager to assist their father on his cases, but often had uncovered mysteries of their own, starting with *The Tower Treasure*, and most recently the baffling *Short-Wave Mystery*.

Frank stood up. "Well, we have an errand to do." He pulled the key they had found at the scene of the accident from his pocket. "Look at this, Dad," he said. "Strange, isn't it?"

"It's odd all right," the detective remarked, examining the ornamental piece of metal. "It must fit a very unusual lock. Where did you get it?"

Frank filled his father in on their adventure, then asked, "Do you know the Mead place?"

"No, I don't."

"Well, we'll go over and see if someone's home."

"Good idea. On the way you can drop off this envelope for Chief Collig, okay?"

"Sure thing, Dad." Frank took the envelope and the boys left.

At police headquarters they found Chief Collig at the teletype machine, scanning the latest reports.

"Hi, fellows," he greeted them, sitting back in his chair. He was a vigorous, middle-aged man with iron-gray hair, who worked closely with the Hardys on their various cases. "What's up?"

Frank handed him the envelope. "Dad asked us to deliver this." He paused for a moment, then asked, "Do you happen to know the Mead place?"

"Yes. Why?"

Frank told how they had met John Mead and found the odd key after he had driven away.

"There's something funny going on here," the chief said slowly. "John Mead has been dead for five years and his house has been closed ever since!"

Frank and Joe stared in amazement. "But we saw—" Joe began.

"I don't know who the man was," Collig said firmly, "but it couldn't have been John Mead. He locked up his house for the winter five years ago and headed for Florida. He and his chauffeur were killed in an automobile accident on the way. No one else lived in the house."

"Perhaps a son—" Frank suggested.

Collig shook his head. "Mead was a bachelor. There was no will, and apparently no relative to claim the estate. So it's been vacant ever since his death."

Their conversation was suddenly interrupted by a telephone call. While waiting for the chief to finish speaking, Frank and Joe discussed the strange situation. If no one lived at the Mead place, who was the man they had met on the road?

"Maybe a con man," Joe suggested.

"He didn't look like one," Frank mused.

"That doesn't mean anything."

"You're right. I say we go over there and check the place out."

When Chief Collig finished his telephone conversation, the boys told him their plan.

"Tell you what," the chief replied, "I'll send one of my men with you. Somehow I have the feeling that there's something very wrong about this whole thing and I don't want you to go alone." He turned to the intercom and pressed a button. A moment later he spoke into the transmitter.

"Riley, are you busy? I want you to take a trip with Frank and Joe Hardy before you go on your beat." The chief waited for an answer, then said, "Fine. They'll be down right away."

The Hardys thanked Chief Collig and hurried to the door.

"Let me know what you find," the chief called after them.

Con Riley was no stranger to the Hardy boys. They had worked with him on past mysteries.

"So we're taking a pleasure jaunt together," he said, smiling, when they met him at the front desk. The three walked quickly down the front steps and got into the boys' convertible.

During the ride Frank explained about John Mead and the unusual key.

"That's weird," Riley commented, shaking his head.

About twenty minutes out of Bayport, Frank turned off the highway and followed a side road which paralleled Barmet Bay. They drove around to the north shore, and presently came upon two large stone pillars covered with vines. The name MEAD was carved on one.

As they turned into the driveway, Joe said, "The place looks deserted to me."

A short distance ahead of them was a clump of trees, around which the driveway wound to the stone mansion. The imposing house at the end of the deeply rutted and overgrown road stood about two hundred feet from the water, commanding an unobstructed view of Barmet Bay.

"Quite a place! Too bad it's so run-down," Riley mused, noting the closed shutters and uncut, weed-covered lawn.

Frank pulled up close to the front entrance and parked. "Now let's see what the inside is like," he said, getting out of the car.

The three strode up the wide stone steps, to the massive front door. Frank took the strange-looking key from his pocket. Suddenly he exclaimed in amazement:

"There's no knob on the door!"

The others stared in disbelief. "Frank," Joe said, "there's not even a keyhole!"

CHAPTER II

The Battered Dory

FRANK, Joe, and Con Riley stared in puzzlement at the heavily carved door.

"This is ridiculous," Frank said. "There must be a way to open it!"

"Maybe it's a swinging door," Riley suggested. He pressed against it, but it did not budge.

"Let's have a look at the other entrances," Frank suggested.

The Mead mansion had four outside doors, one on each side. All were ornate, but like the main entrance had no visible knobs, locks, or keyholes.

"What do you make of this?" Frank asked Joe, still shaking his head.

"Looks as if this key doesn't belong to the house after all," Joe muttered.

"It might not even have been dropped by our alleged Mr. Mead," Frank observed. He was thoughtful for a moment, glancing up at the windows. They were shuttered and appeared to be without hinges or fasteners.

"One thing is for sure," he continued. "The architect who designed this place didn't like hardware. There must be a keyhole hidden in the carved designs on the doors. Let's examine them more carefully."

"You start," Joe replied. "I want to go down to that boathouse and look it over. Seems like a pretty nice one from here."

He hurried along a narrow path that led from the mansion to the water. A tangle of bushes and large overgrown flower beds indicated that the grounds had once been beautiful; now they were badly neglected.

The boathouse was locked. Its side door had no knob, keyhole, or other means of opening it. The two windows had closed shutters like those on the house.

"Wonder if there's a boat inside," Joe mused. But there was no way of finding out except by swimming under the large rolling door on the water side.

A honking came from the main house and Joe ran back to find Officer Riley with his hand on the horn.

"Sorry, boys," he said as Frank joined them. "I have to get back on my beat!" He added, "I checked the back door and found absolutely nothing!"

"I found nothing on the east side door," Frank reported, and then Joe told them about his quick survey of the boathouse.

The Hardys were reluctant to leave, but had no alternative. They climbed into the convertible and headed for Bayport.

When they stopped at headquarters to let Riley off, they were surprised to see their father coming down the steps. They waited to tell him about the strange doors at the Mead mansion, whose owner was reportedly dead.

"Most unusual," he commented. "We'll certainly have to look into the matter. No knobs or keyholes, eh?" He gazed into space for a moment, then added, "Let's talk it over later. Right now I'd like to borrow your car. Mine's being repaired at the Acme Garage, and I must see a man over in Henryville."

Frank and Joe got out and started for home on foot. They took a short cut that brought them to the back of their property. Suddenly Frank caught Joe's arm and whispered:

"Look!"

"What's up?"

Frank pointed. Crouching at the back door of the Hardy home was a man, apparently picking the lock!

As Joe started to run, Frank grabbed him by the arm. "Hold on!" he warned in a low voice.

"And let the thief get away?"

"If you rush him, he will get away. Let's sneak up on him!"

Tiptoeing swiftly across the yard, the boys reached the picklock without being heard.

"Say, what's the idea?" Frank cried out.

Startled, the man jumped and turned to face the Hardys. Bracing themselves for a fight, they were astounded when he made no move to run. Instead, he asked insolently:

"Who do you think you are?"

"We live here," Joe replied. "And it looks as if we got here just in time, too."

"I suppose you think I'm a burglar," said the stranger. "You Hardys think everybody's a crook. Well, I got a perfect right to be here, so run along and catch a thief somewhere else."

Frank's eyes flashed, and Joe could hardly keep his fists under control.

The thin, sneering young man went on, "Mrs. Hardy ordered this lock changed, and I'm here to do it."

The boys were taken aback. Although this was a plausible answer, it struck them as peculiar, for their mother had not mentioned having any locks changed, and they knew she was not at home.

"Who sent you here?" Frank asked.

"Ben Whittaker. Does that satisfy you?"

Frank and Joe knew old Ben well. He had been Bayport's leading locksmith and hardware dealer

A man was picking the lock on the Hardys' back door

for many years. They wondered how he could tolerate such a disagreeable employee.

Still suspicious, Joe asked the fellow his name and was told it was Mike Batton. Frank stayed out with the workman while Joe went inside and telephoned the Whittaker shop. Ben answered. Yes, Whittaker reported, Mike Batton worked for him, and on his desk pad was an order to change the lock on the Hardys' back door at once.

"Will you please describe Mike Batton," Joe requested.

Mr. Whittaker's description fitted the young man perfectly. Joe went outdoors again.

"Okay, Batton," he said. "You win. But I'm sure there's some mistake. Since you haven't started your work yet, don't bother with the lock."

"That's okay with me," the workman growled, and went up the walk to the street without looking back.

"What did you find out?" Frank asked his brother.

Joe told him what Ben Whittaker had said, and added, "His story seems to be on the level, but I'm still not satisfied. I wish Mother would come home so we could ask her."

But Mrs. Hardy did not return, and after eating lunch, the boys became impatient.

"Why don't we go down and see Mr. Whittaker?" Frank suggested. "I'd like to find out more about Batton. There's just no sense in anyone trying to change a lock without even opening the door!"

"Right!" agreed Joe. "And say, we might ask Mr. Whittaker about the Mead place. Maybe he's seen the strange doors there, and knows whether the key we have fits any hidden locks in them."

The Hardys started down the street. They had gone only three blocks when their chubby friend Chet Morton jumped out of a yellow sedan which stopped briefly and then went on. He was munching an apple.

"Hi, fellows," he greeted them. "I was on my way to your house. Phil gave me a ride. Going anywhere special?"

"Well, sort of," Joe replied. "Why?"

"Put it off," Chet insisted importantly. "I've got something to show you."

"What is it?"

"Come with me to Water Street and you'll see," Chet said mysteriously.

Frank winked at Joe. They were always secretly amused by their friend's great enthusiasm for any new interest. Chet lived on a farm just outside of Bayport, and when he was not helping the Hardys on a mystery, he was constantly developing any one of a dozen different hobbies.

Frank and Joe wondered what Chet was up to this time.

At Water Street their friend turned down a

lane leading to the shore of Barmet Bay. Frank and Joe followed as he walked onto a dilapidated dock, stopping at the edge.

"There she is," Chet said proudly, pointing. "Pretty swell, eh?"

Chained and padlocked to a pile was a heavy dory. It was nicked and scarred, and badly in need of paint. Altogether, the boat did not look very seaworthy. It had a motor, but the Hardys guessed from its age that it would not run.

"My craft's not as fancy as the *Sleuth*," Chet declared, "but I can go fishing now any time I want."

The *Sleuth* was the Hardys' sleek, powerful speedboat. They had paid for it with reward money they had received for successfully solving a past mystery.

"Do *you* own this boat?" Frank asked in astonishment.

"Yep. Bought 'er only an hour ago. She's the *Bloodhound!*"

"How about a ride up the bay?" Joe asked, grinning.

"Sure thing," Chet answered enthusiastically. "You fellows start the engine while I get the oars. They're in that boathouse over there. Came with the *Bloodhound* in case of emergency."

As their friend ran off, Frank and Joe inspected the ancient motor, which had to be cranked by hand. They turned it over until their arms ached. Then they tried priming the engine with gasoline from the spare can, but it refused even to sputter.

When Chet returned and heard the bad news, he did not seem at all downcast. The boy said confidently that with a little work, the motor would go.

"Can't understand it, though," he remarked. "That fellow assured me it was in good running order."

"What fellow?" asked Joe.

"The one who sold me the boat." After a moment's reflection, Chet added, "But I suppose I should have tried it first to see that everything was all right."

Frank and Joe made no comment. They knew that Chet was a bright boy, but usually his hindsight was better than his foresight.

"Let's go for a ride, anyway," Chet urged.

It was agreed that the boys would take turns rowing. Chet started.

Presently Frank, seated in the bow, noticed a built-in metal box. He tried to raise the lid, but it was locked.

"What's in here?" he asked.

"Don't know," Chet replied. "Haven't looked yet."

"Got a key?"

Sheepishly the boy admitted that none had

come with the boat. He said he would be sure to ask for one when the man brought the registration and bill of sale.

"When are you going to see the fellow?" Joe asked.

"In an hour. He had to get the papers at the bank," Chet answered, starting to puff. "How about one of you taking a turn at the oars?"

Frank got up to take Chet's place. Suddenly he was thrown off balance by the rocking of the boat. The water, which had been calm when they started out, was now very choppy. Waves slapped furiously against the side of the *Bloodhound*.

Chet quickly pulled the boat around so the next wave would strike it head-on. But the old dory gave a convulsive shudder and a torrent of water came rushing into it.

"We've sprung a leak!" Joe cried.

He had hardly finished the sentence when two of the seams split wide open, and water gushed through them.

"Jump!" Frank warned. "Jump!"

As the dory began to sink, the Hardys dived overboard. Chet seemed paralyzed for the moment. Only when the water reached his waist did he rouse himself and leap from the boat.

Grimly the three set out for shore, as the *Bloodhound* sank to the bottom of Barmet Bay in twelve feet of water. Swimming was difficult in the rough sea but finally they reached the dock.

Chet sat down and held his head in his hands. He was sad and chagrined, and almost exhausted.

"It's a shame," Frank said. "Wish we could help you, Chet."

"Guess there's nothing we can do," the boy muttered. "All my hard-earned money gone."

"Maybe not. The fellow who sold you the dory ought to make good on it."

"You're right!" Chet cried, jumping up. "When he comes, I'm going to tell him his old boat wasn't worth a cent!"

Although the boys waited until their clothes dried, the stranger, whom Chet described as a dark-haired, stocky man of about thirty, did not appear. Chet had become more dejected by the moment, but suddenly he brightened.

"You can find that guy for me!" he said to the Hardys. "You're detectives."

"Why do you need a detective to find him?" Joe asked.

" 'Cause I—'cause I don't know who he is!"

"You don't know? You mean you bought a boat without finding out the owner's name?"

" 'Fraid so," Chet said sadly.

"Maybe the fellow didn't even own the boat. He might have rented it—or even stolen it," Frank mused.

Chet turned pale. "Then I—I'd be liable!"

"We'd better find him," Joe said determinedly.

The old man in charge of the boathouse was

very sympathetic when he heard their story. He scratched his head thoughtfully, then said:

"Mebbe I kin help you at that."

"You can?" Chet cried. "How?"

"Seems to me the feller that sold you the boat said he was agoin' to git one o' them express buses out o' Bayport just about now."

"Wow!" yelled Joe. "Maybe we can catch him!"

The three boys ran all the way to the bus terminal. Chet was red-faced and puffing by the time they reached the building, only to find that the bus had pulled out a few minutes before.

"What's the next stop?" Joe inquired at the ticket office.

"Lewiston."

Joe reported this to the others, adding, "Lewiston's ten miles from here."

"Can't do anything without a car," Frank said.

"We might use Dad's," Joe suggested.

"We must find that man!" Chet urged. "I'll buy you gas, and I'll—"

The Acme garage was in the next block and the three boys raced there. Fortunately Mr. Hardy's car was ready. With Frank at the wheel, they drove off at once. Reaching the outskirts of Bayport, they headed westward. Just as they came into Lewiston, the boys caught up with the bus.

"You get on, Chet, and find your man," Frank

suggested as the driver stopped in the center of town.

"Wh-what'll I say to him?" Chet asked help-lessly.

"You want your money back, don't you?" Joe asked. "Hurry!"

Excited and worried, Chet got out of the car and boarded the bus.

CHAPTER III

Disturbing Developments

"Maybe we ought to go help Chet," Frank said to Joe, observing that their friend seemed to be having an argument with the bus driver.

The man had no intention of delaying his trip while the inquisitive youth looked over the passengers.

"If you want to go back there, pay your fare!" the man demanded.

"But I don't want to ride," the stout boy said. "I just want to see—"

"Give me the fare or get off!"

Just then Frank appeared at the door of the bus. He inquired in a long-winded manner what the next stop would be, and how often the express buses ran. Chet took the cue: His friend was trying to gain time for him. He stepped farther back into the bus. In his excitement the stout boy came down hard on a woman's foot.

"Ow!" she cried out angrily, attracting everybody's attention.

The driver turned to Chet. "Hey, you! Get off this bus!"

In despair Chet, who had not yet seen all the passengers, was about to produce the fare when Joe put one foot up on the platform. He pretended to push Frank aside, and asked the driver:

"What time do you get to Ellsville?"

"This bus doesn't go to Ellsville."

"Then how do I get there?" Joe looked puzzled.

The driver was in a rather bad humor by now. "Guess you'll have to walk," he answered gruffly, then turned to Chet. "Are you riding or getting off?"

"I'm getting off. And thanks!"

The three boys hopped to the curb as the driver slammed the door and pulled away.

They walked slowly toward their car. Chet reported sadly that the man who had sold him the dory was not on the bus.

"What'll I do now?" he asked anxiously.

Frank placed a hand on his friend's shoulder. "What say we get the *Sleuth* and inquire up and down Barmet Bay about your boat? Maybe we can find out where it came from."

"Great!" Chet said, looking relieved. "Let's go!"

They headed toward Bayport. Reaching the

shore, they drove directly to the Hardys' private dock.

After parking the car and opening the seaward doors of the boathouse, the three climbed aboard the sleek motorboat.

"Which way shall we go?" asked Joe as soon as they were all seated. He took the wheel and headed the *Sleuth* into deeper water.

"I'd say toward the ocean," Frank replied. "Chet's boat was a fishing dory, and probably was owned by someone who went out to sea in her."

"Hear that, Chet?" Joe said with a wink. "Frank's got his old logic working again."

"Wish I had his brains," Chet replied.

Frank laughed, and the craft sped up the coast. The boys inquired at every house and dock for a mile along the waterfront, but no one knew anything about the dory.

"Let's head for the other side and see what we can find out," Chet suggested.

Joe steered the *Sleuth* across the bay. As he neared the opposite shore, he called attention to the property which lay just ahead.

"It's the Mead place," he explained to Chet. "We haven't had time to tell you about the mystery we ran into this morning."

Chet listened wide-eyed as the Hardys told him about the car which had lost a wheel and the driver who had used the name of a dead man, and the strange key. At this point in the story Frank suddenly cried out, "I've lost it!"

"Lost what?" Chet asked.

"The key!" Frank was frantically searching through his pockets.

Joe stared at his brother anxiously. Finally he said, "Maybe you left it at home."

"No. I wish I had," Frank answered, giving a groan. "I guess it fell from my pocket when we dived out of Chet's boat."

"Well, it probably doesn't belong to the Mead doors, anyway," Joe said.

"Just the same, I wish I hadn't lost it," Frank muttered.

"I'd like to see those doors," Chet announced. "Let's tie up and have a look."

Joe cut the motor and allowed the *Sleuth* to drift to shore. Here he made it fast to the dock adjoining the Mead boathouse. The boys got out and walked to the side door.

"Wow!" Chet exclaimed. "This really *is* a mystery! Even the boathouse door has no keyhole or knob."

"Wait until you see the mansion," Joe said with a grin. "Come on!"

The Hardys led the way and their friend looked in bewilderment at the heavily carved rear door.

"Are they all this fancy?" he wanted to know.

"Yes. Each has a different design, though," Frank replied.

"And none has any apparent way to get in," Joe added. "Queer, eh?"

As the boys rounded the house to inspect the front entrance, they heard a car coming along the driveway. Frank and Joe thought it might be the man who called himself John Mead, so they waited. But the car was not Mead's. Before the boys could get a look at the driver he backed around the curve and turned back.

"Well, what do you make of that?" cried Joe.

"Either somebody lost his way, or didn't want to meet us," Frank replied.

He ran forward, trying to catch a glimpse of the car's license plate, but it was almost out of sight. When it reached the highway, it roared off in the direction of Bayport.

Frank glanced at his watch, noting the time for possible future reference. "Four-thirty," he stated.

"Oh, oh," Chet cried, "I'm supposed to meet my mother at five downtown!"

The three boys hurried to the boathouse and jumped into the *Sleuth*. Frank sent it skimming across the water, and ten minutes later they alighted in Bayport.

After housing the *Sleuth,* the trio got into Mr. Hardy's car and Frank took Chet to the place where he was to meet his mother. Luckily Mrs. Morton was not waiting yet.

Chet jumped out and waved good-by. "See you

tomorrow, fellows. And don't forget to work on my case!"

"Don't worry," Frank called out to his friend, then headed home.

Mrs. Hardy, a slim, attractive woman, was in the kitchen mixing batter for popovers, and from the oven came the appetizing aroma of roast beef.

"Smells good," Frank said, grinning. "Where'd you learn to cook?"

"That's my secret," his mother replied with a smile.

"Speaking of secrets," Joe began, "I wish you wouldn't keep so many to yourself."

"What do you mean?" Mrs. Hardy was puzzled.

The boys told her of the man who had been about to change the back-door lock, and that they had stopped him.

"Well, I'm certainly glad you did!" their mother exclaimed. "There must be a mistake. I didn't phone Ben Whittaker."

"We didn't think you had," replied Frank. "Let's go right down there and find out what that guy Batton is up to. Come on, Joe."

"Okay, but be back in time for dinner."

"We will."

A few minutes later Frank and Joe parked in front of Ben Whittaker's store. He was just closing the shop, but smiled at the boys as he let them in.

"Has Mike Batton gone for the day?" Frank asked.

"Yes. In fact, he didn't come back here after he went out on some errands a few hours ago."

"Mr. Whittaker," Joe asked, "have you found Batton to be entirely honest?"

The locksmith looked startled. "Why—ah—yes," he answered. "What's on your mind, boys?"

They told the elderly man about finding his assistant changing the back-door lock on the Hardy house without authorization.

Mr. Whittaker looked concerned and went immediately to his desk.

"Here's the order," he said, holding up a pad.

"May I see it?" Frank asked.

Whittaker handed him the pad. Written on it was "Hardy—back-door lock" and under it "Mrs. Eccles." Frank suggested that the locksmith call Mrs. Eccles to see if she had left an order to have her lock changed.

Mr. Whittaker apprehensively made the call. His expression became more grave as he spoke with Mrs. Eccles. When he finally hung up, he said in a weary voice:

"She's very upset. She never ordered any lockwork either, but her lock was changed while she was out shopping. And when she returned, two hundred dollars was missing from her desk drawer!"

Mr. Whittaker paced up and down, completely baffled. "I can't understand it. Batton came with excellent references."

"How long has he worked here?" Frank asked.

"I hired him just about a week ago. Needed help badly and—" The man's voice trailed off.

"Where does he live?" Joe asked.

"In a boardinghouse on Dover Street. I'll call him."

The woman who answered the phone said Batton was out and had left word he would not be back until late that evening.

The locksmith looked strained and tired, so the boys left. "We'll call you if we hear anything, Mr. Whittaker," Frank said. "I'm sure there's an explanation."

"Yes. My employee is a thief," Mr. Whittaker said sadly and locked the shop door. "Thanks, boys."

Both Frank and Joe felt uneasy as they drove home, and were more suspicious of Batton than before. One mistake might happen, but hardly two of the same kind. And what about the money?

"What I can't understand," said Joe, "is this. If Batton is a thief, why did he pick our house? The Eccles are pretty wealthy, but we're not."

"It's a puzzler, all right," Frank agreed. "I'm still inclined to think that Batton never intended to put a new lock on our door; he just planned to get into the house. But why? In any event, he covered himself nicely with that false order on the phone pad."

When the boys reached home they learned that

Mr. Hardy would not return until the next morning. Mrs. Hardy and her sons sat down to dinner and during the meal Frank and Joe told her everything that had happened that day.

"Looks as if you have two or three mysteries on your hands," their mother said with a smile when they had finished their report. "Which one will you work on first?"

"All of them at once," Joe replied with a grin.

"Sometime tomorrow," Frank said, "I want to dive for that lost key. I meant to ask Mr. Whittaker if he knew anything about the Mead place, but didn't have the heart to. He was so upset."

"You have another big day ahead of you," Mrs. Hardy said. "Better go to bed early."

Frank and Joe followed her advice, and their mother also retired at ten o'clock. It was past midnight that she was awakened by the doorbell.

She called out to the boys, who had heard it too and had come from their room. "I'll see who it is," Joe offered, putting on his robe and bedroom slippers.

As he spoke, the bell rang again. This time the caller kept a finger on the button. Frank and Joe hurried downstairs.

Mrs. Hardy was right behind them and warned the boys to be cautious. Before opening the door, Frank snapped on the porch light and looked out the glass panel.

Joe peered over his shoulder. "Do you know

her?" he asked his brother, pointing to the visitor.

Frank shook his head.

Outside stood a strange woman, fidgeting nervously. She wore a faded pink hat over her short blond hair. A black coat had been thrown carelessly over her slim shoulders. As Frank slowly opened the door, she pushed it in excitedly.

"Where's Mr. Hardy?" she cried in a shrill, hysterical voice. "I've got to see him right away!"

CHAPTER IV

The Traffic Signal Clue

THE distraught woman continued frantically, "I've got to see Mr. Hardy. Right away. Where is he?"

Mrs. Hardy turned on a light in the living room and led the visitor to a chair.

"Please sit down," she said kindly. "Mr. Hardy isn't here at the moment, but perhaps we can help you."

"Oh, no! Only Mr. Hardy can help me," the stranger cried. "He's got to help my Lenny. I'll spend every cent of my savings if I have to."

"Lenny is your son?" Frank asked.

"Yes. He's a good boy. In all his eighteen years he never did wrong."

"Where is he?" Joe inquired.

"That's just it. I don't know."

"Have you been to the police?"

The woman gave a shriek. "Police? I should say

not! They wouldn't understand. They might put Lenny in jail. That never happened to a Stryker and it's not gonna happen now!"

As the woman paused for breath, Frank inquired if she was Mrs. Stryker. The caller nodded, adding that she was a widow and Lenny was her only child.

"I'm sorry you're in trouble," said Mrs. Hardy. "When Mr. Hardy returns tomorrow—"

The caller wrung her hands. "Tomorrow? I was hoping he could do something tonight. You see, I got a message from Lenny just a little while ago, and something ought to be done right away. He said the gang nearly got caught, and he'd been shot in the leg."

"Shot!" chorused the three Hardys, and Frank added, "What Lenny needs is a doctor."

"He needs a detective too!" Mrs. Stryker moaned. She did not know where Lenny was, and was afraid he would not receive proper care. "That's why I want Mr. Hardy to find him."

"Did your son give you any hint about where he is?" Joe asked eagerly.

"I think so. I'll tell you all I know."

The boys leaned forward in their chairs, waiting intently for the woman's story. She told them her son had acted mysteriously lately, and that she suspected he had fallen into bad company. He had gone out earlier that night. Then, at eleven-thirty he had telephoned, saying he had been shot.

"And you don't have any idea whom he went out with?" Frank inquired.

"No. But Lenny mumbled some funny words on the phone," Mrs. Stryker explained. "Two of them sounded like 'secret panel.' Then the connection was cut off."

Secret panel!

Frank and Joe looked at each other. It was a clue, all right, but where could one start to investigate? Though the boys quizzed Mrs. Stryker for fifteen minutes, she could shed no more light on the subject. At last she stood up to go, disappointed because the Hardys could give her no immediate help.

"But you *promise* to tell Mr. Hardy about it the minute he comes in tomorrow?" she begged.

"Yes, we will," Frank assured her.

The woman wrote down her address and went out into the night.

"Poor soul," Mrs. Hardy said, and all three went upstairs and back to bed.

Fenton Hardy arrived home before breakfast the next morning and listened attentively to the story of Lenny Stryker. His face grew grave.

"It seems this boy has really gotten himself mixed up with a rough crowd."

"You sound as if you know who they are, Dad," Frank remarked.

"I have a suspicion," Mr. Hardy began. "Come on. I'll tell you about it over breakfast."

As the family sat down at the dining-room table, they heard the screech of brakes and the slam of a car door. Moments later the bell rang.

Frank answered it and was surprised to see their father's close friend Dr. William Gardner.

"Is your Dad home?" Dr. Gardner asked quickly. He was middle-aged and seemed very agitated. As Mr. Hardy came into the hall, he went on, "I've just talked to the police, Fenton, and Chief Collig thought you ought to know, too, about what happened."

"Suppose we go to my study, Bill."

The detective led the way upstairs and motioned Frank and Joe to follow.

"Thank you," Dr. Gardner said and sat down in a chair. "My troubles are over; at least I hope they are. But something must be done to punish the culprits." He lowered his voice. "Last night I was kidnapped!"

"What!" Frank exclaimed.

"Yes," the doctor went on. "I was leaving the hospital about ten-thirty when two men came up and ordered me into a car at gunpoint. They promised I wouldn't be harmed if I did as I was told."

"What did they look like?" Joe inquired.

"I have no idea," Dr. Gardner replied. "Everything happened too fast. I really didn't notice."

He told how he had been blindfolded, then driven some place in the car, forced to get out and enter a building. When the blindfold was removed, he found himself in a room with several masked men.

"They were taking no chances," remarked Mr. Hardy.

"Right. Even the patient I was to treat had his face covered," Dr. Gardner went on.

"Where was the bullet?" Frank asked excitedly.

"In his right leg."

The Hardys exchanged quick glances. Could the patient have been Lenny Stryker? To their questions the physician replied that the man's leg was the only part of his body he had seen uncovered, and that there was no distinguishing mark on it which could be used as a means of identification.

"All I can say is that he's very young, and has a lot of grit. He didn't cry out once!"

"What did the room look like, Bill?" Mr. Hardy questioned. "Would you say you got into it through a panel?"

"I could see very little in the room. It was dark except around the patient. One of the men held a lamp so I could work," Dr. Gardner replied. "It seemed as if the room had no windows, or if there were any, they were well covered. As for the secret panel, I really couldn't say."

"Tell me about how long you spent riding to and from the place, and if you noticed anything unusual on the way," Mr. Hardy requested.

Dr. Gardner was thoughtful for a minute. "I don't know how accurate I may be," he mused, "but I'd say we went about thirty miles an hour. One thing does come to mind. About ten minutes before reaching the place, we stopped briefly."

"What for?"

"A traffic light, I think. I noticed a humming sound as we waited—almost a singing noise. It could have been the signal. Sometimes they do hum, you know. It was the same on the trip back to the hospital, where they finally let me go. Is this information at all helpful?"

"It's a good clue," Mr. Hardy said enthusiastically. "Suppose you follow it, boys."

"All right," Joe answered. "First thing this morning!"

Dr. Gardner wished the Hardys luck on the search. After he had gone, Mr. Hardy called Chief Collig, who told him that he had advised all the hospitals in the area to warn their staffs to be on guard. The police chief said he would inform the Hardys the minute he heard of any new development. Then the detective turned to his sons.

"Stop by Mrs. Stryker's house sometime today and tell her I'll try to find Lenny," he said. "It looks as if he may be involved with the same gang I'm hunting for."

Frank and Joe stared in surprise.

"There's a wanted criminal by the name of Whitey Masco, who's been in hiding for a long time," Mr. Hardy went on. "He was involved in some bank robberies and is suspected to be the mastermind of a big gang."

"What makes you think Lenny has anything to do with him?"

"Last night another appliance warehouse was broken into. Just as the thieves were leaving, the watchman, whom they had knocked out earlier, regained consciousness and saw someone running away. He fired a shot, and it's just possible he hit Lenny Stryker."

"Why didn't the thieves take the guard's gun?"

Mr. Hardy smiled. "Maybe they gave that job to Lenny and he couldn't handle it. Well, we'd better eat breakfast and start on our projects."

He led the way back to the dining room. "I have an appointment with an FBI man, and you have—"

Just then someone slammed the kitchen screen door, and a cheery voice called out, "Hello."

It was Chet. He sniffed the air, looked at a platter of bacon and eggs, and grinned.

"Hi, Chet. You're just in time," said Joe. "I bet you haven't had a thing to eat for an hour."

Chet pretended not to hear the gibe. He walked into the dining room and drew up a chair.

"Good morning, everyone," he said brightly.

As the family greeted him, he went on, "I've had my breakfast, but I could eat one of those bananas." He reached into the fruit basket. Everyone laughed.

The Hardys were just finishing breakfast when the doorbell rang. Frank went to answer it. To his surprise he found his Aunt Gertrude standing outside.

"Well, let me in!" she said, giving him a quick kiss before he picked up her suitcase. "Where is everybody?"

Without waiting for an answer, the unpredictable Miss Hardy went on, "They're still at the breakfast table, I'll bet!" She strode into the dining room and greeted the others.

"Laura, how can you stand to have meals at all hours? Well, things will be different now that I'm here!"

Frank, Joe, and even Chet knew this only too well. Aunt Gertrude, though she loved her famous brother's family, always made a point of trying to improve their habits.

The tall, energetic spinster ruled with an iron fist, at least on the surface, and the boys had learned not to argue with her.

"Hello, Gertrude," Mrs. Hardy said with a smile as her husband got up to greet his sister. "We didn't expect you home until tomorrow. Tell us, how did you get here? We would have come for you if we had known your plans."

Miss Hardy, who had been away for two weeks

visiting friends, said that she had decided to return earlier than planned.

"I called a couple of times from the airport, but couldn't get you. Your telephone was forever busy. So I took a taxi. Thought I'd surprise you."

"Well, let me help you unpack."

Joe picked up his aunt's suitcase and followed the two women to Aunt Gertrude's room, when the telephone rang. Frank answered.

It was Ben Whittaker, the locksmith. "Can you come over right away?" He sounded distressed.

"What's up?" Frank wanted to know.

"I'll tell you when you get here. Please hurry!"

"Okay." Frank hung up, and when Joe came downstairs, told him of the strange conversation.

"Well, what are we waiting for? Let's go!" Joe said.

Briefly, Frank explained their errand to his parents. Chet had not eaten all he would have liked to, but he thought it wise to leave with his pals. Any moment now Miss Hardy might start trying to reform his eating habits!

The three boys went outside and scrambled into the convertible. A moment later they were on their way. When they arrived at Mr. Whittaker's shop, they found the locksmith in a state of extreme anxiety.

"Mike Batton hasn't come back. I phoned his house, and they told me that he's moved out. Nobody knows where he's gone!"

CHAPTER V

A Futile Search

FRANK and Joe listened to the shopkeeper's surprising announcement and were startled when he continued:

"Even worse, I've discovered that all the money we took in yesterday is missing from the cash register!"

"Oh, oh," Joe said. "Looks as if Batton is a thief, all right."

"Yes," the locksmith went on. "I've notified the police. But the thing I'm most upset about is that my reputation is at stake. I've been in business for forty years and nobody ever had any reason to question my integrity before. And it's all Mike Batton's doing!"

"What happened?" Chet asked.

"Mrs. Eccles phoned a few minutes ago and wants her money back. Furthermore, Batton changed another lock yesterday, for the Petersons, and they report that a valuable bracelet and a hundred dollars in cash are missing!"

Frank suggested that surely his customers would realize he was not responsible for the loss of their valuables. To take the worried man's mind off his troubles, Frank asked him if he knew John Mead, who had owned the mansion that had no locks.

"I did," Mr. Whittaker replied. "Nice man. That was a terrible accident. He and the chauffeur were killed instantly."

"Please tell us about him," Joe said.

"Well, at one time he was a partner in a big hardware concern in New York," the locksmith revealed. "He once told me he vowed to build himself a house without a single lock or keyhole when he retired. He was so tired of looking at locks he never wanted to see another one in his whole life!"

Whittaker went on to say that he had spent several evenings at the Mead mansion with the hardware manufacturer, discussing locksmithing problems. Mead had been extremely clever and inventive, but a little eccentric. He had never mentioned having any family, and no will had been found after his death. So far as Whittaker knew, no one had claimed the estate.

"Don't any of the doors at the mansion have locks on them?" Chet asked in awe.

"Oh, yes," Mr. Whittaker said, smiling. "They all do, but they're cleverly concealed."

"Do you know where?"

"No. He installed them himself."

After thanking the locksmith for the information and agreeing to do what they could to help in the search for Mike Batton, the boys left the shop.

"Now what?" Chet asked.

"We could go over to Mrs. Stryker and see if she's heard any more from Lenny," Frank suggested.

"Good idea," Joe agreed. "Want to come along, Chet?"

"Sure do."

Frank drove to a shabby, run-down section of Bayport. They located the Strykers' apartment building, and Chet stayed in the car while Frank and Joe went inside. They found the place to be clean and tidy. Lenny's mother greeted them.

"Have you any news of my boy?" she asked, her eyes lighting up hopefully.

Frank shook his head. "I'm afraid not. We do have a clue, though. A doctor came to our house this morning and said he had been kidnapped last night to take care of a young man who had been shot in the leg."

"It must have been Lenny!" the woman cried out. "Where is he? I'll go at once."

"Dr. Gardner couldn't tell us where he had

been taken because he was blindfolded. However, he gave us a good clue. Don't worry, Mrs. Stryker. The doctor said the boy he treated was all right. If it's Lenny, we'll find him."

"Does the name Whitey Masco mean anything to you?" Joe asked.

The woman shook her head. "Nothing. Who is he?"

"Just a name that came up. Probably has nothing to do with Lenny," Frank assured her. Then the boys left.

When they reached the car, Chet was not in it. They spied him at a nearby street intersection. He was looking up intently at the traffic light, his head cocked to one side. When he saw Frank and Joe, he ran toward them.

"Well, *that* one doesn't sing," Chet declared as he got into the car.

"Let's investigate some others," Joe said.

The three boys drove without success from one traffic light to another. Just as they were about to stop for the day, Frank cried, "Listen!"

A traffic signal hung high above the pavement at the intersection of two wide streets. A distinct humming sound came from it as the automatic timer changed the lights.

"Now we're getting somewhere!" Joe cried excitedly. "Dr. Gardner said he was driven for about ten minutes from a singing signal. Which direction shall we take first?"

It was decided to go north at the rate of thirty miles an hour, as the physician had estimated.

"Stop!" Joe called.

Chet's face broke into a broad smile. They were directly in front of a roadside restaurant.

"Well, fellows," he said, "you two can go hunting for kidnapping gangsters and secret panels all you like. I'm going to eat!"

A sign advertising lunches and dinners swung from a post in front of a small white cottage. Flowered curtains hung at the windows and rose-bushes were in bloom along the walk.

"Doesn't look like a hideout for thieves," said Joe, disappointed.

Frank pointed out that the attractive front might be only a cover for some sinister doings inside. He insisted they find out, adding:

"Guess we all could eat, anyway. Let's go in. I'll telephone and tell Mother we won't be home for lunch."

The woman who owned the restaurant prepared a delicious meal for the boys, while they looked around. They saw the entire cottage, even the basement, for the owner proudly showed them her preserve closet. There was nothing the least bit suspicious about the house.

As the boys were driving away some time later, Chet, almost too full to speak, congratulated Frank on his cleverness in arriving at such an inviting destination.

"Only our stop didn't net us anything except a good meal," Frank reminded him.

He drove back to the humming traffic light, then headed in a westerly direction. At the end of ten minutes, the boys came to a ball field. They returned once more to the signal, and Joe pointed out that the easterly direction would take them directly into the bay.

"Our last chance to find out where Dr. Gardner was taken is to drive south," he remarked.

As they reached a congested business section of Bayport ten minutes later, Frank suggested that they separate. "Joe, suppose you take this street. I'll go over to Wallace. Chet, how about you taking Schuyler Street?"

Chet started off enthusiastically, but after being shooed out of a laundry, icily dismissed from a beauty shop, and practically thrown out of a soda bottling factory, he was ready to quit. He walked back to the car. Joe, who had had no better luck, was waiting for him.

"Frank must be on a hot trail," Joe decided, when half an hour went by and his brother had not returned.

At that moment Frank was hiding in the dimly lighted cellar of a warehouse. He had followed a tip given to him by a small boy—that rough-looking men had been seen leaving and entering the building with large packages, at all hours of the day and night.

Frank was watching the operator who had just stepped from a freight elevator. Reaching the far wall of the cellar, the man leaned down and evidently worked a catch. A large door slid open and he disappeared behind it. He returned almost immediately, however, closed the door, and went back to the elevator.

As soon as it had clanged upward, Frank came out of his hiding place and approached the sliding door. *Perhaps this was the secret panel!*

He found the catch and slowly pushed against it with his knee. The door opened. The place beyond was in total darkness.

Whipping out his flashlight, Frank played its beam around the room. Then, muttering in disgust, he quickly left the basement. He made his way from the building and returned to the car.

"Did you find anything?" Joe asked eagerly.

"Yes. A huge refrigerator. It was empty except for the elevator operator's lunch!"

The others laughed when Frank related how he had thought Lenny Stryker might be hidden in the warehouse.

"That reminds me," Chet said, looking at his watch. "I'd better go. I have to pick up some groceries on the way home."

Frank sighed. "The humming signal clue seems to have petered out," he declared. "I guess there's no use doing any more about it now."

The Hardys stopped at a supermarket where

Chet made his purchases, then drove their friend home. As they headed toward their own house, Joe had an idea.

"It's still early. Why don't we go for a swim and combine a little business with pleasure?"

"What's on your mind?"

"How about diving for Mr. Mead's key?"

"Swell," Frank agreed. "We'll stop at the house and get our swim trunks."

Frank parked the car in front of their home, instead of going into the garage. Aunt Gertrude, sitting on the porch, remarked about this at once. She wanted to know where the boys were going, and why.

Joe's reply that they were working on a mystery satisfied her for the moment. But when they could not find their swim trunks, and had to ask Miss Hardy about them, she eyed her nephews distrustfully.

"Whoever heard of solving a mystery in a bathing suit!" she scoffed. "I declare, what excuses boys won't think of nowadays to escape doing chores around the house."

Joe and Frank smiled as she found their trunks for them, and with a disapproving look on her face, watched them go off.

Frank drove to the boathouse where the *Sleuth* was moored. He and Joe hung their clothes on hooks, donned their trunks, and headed the craft out into Barmet Bay. It took them some time to

The man disappeared behind the sliding door

locate the place where they thought Chet's ill-fated boat had gone down.

"I'll go over first," Frank offered.

He made a clean, deep dive from the stern of the *Sleuth*. Joe watched the spot where his brother had submerged. When more than a minute had passed and there was no sign of Frank, he became concerned.

Joe leaned far over the side of the boat and looked down into the clear water. Then he stood up and studied the surface of the bay.

Frank was nowhere in sight!

CHAPTER VI

The Strange Symbol

His heart pounding with fright, Joe dived over the side of the boat and into the bay. He went straight to the bottom, and swam around searching for his brother.

Where was Frank?

Finally, when he felt his lungs would burst, Joe had to come up for air. He looked around when his head broke the surface. Still no sign of Frank. Sick at heart, Joe climbed into the *Sleuth*, gazing about frantically.

Suddenly his pulse quickened. In the distance he saw a swimmer cutting the water with smooth, fast strokes. As the figure grew closer, Joe gave a sigh of relief. *Frank!*

Panting, Frank grabbed the side of the boat and scrambled aboard.

"Where have you been?" Joe asked anxiously. "You gave me an awful scare!"

"There's no sign of Chet's dory below us," Frank told him. "So I swam around trying to find it. Guess I came up for air when you dived for me. I went farther than I realized. Sorry I worried you."

"That's okay. Did you see the *Bloodhound?*"

"No, but I'm sure it's somewhere near here."

Joe started the engine of the *Sleuth*. Frank gazed down through the water as they made their way slowly. No sunken boat was visible.

"Guess we'll have to give up," he said with a sigh. "But sure wish I hadn't lost the key. Hey, hold it, Joe!"

"See something?" Joe cut the motor.

Both boys leaned over the side of the *Sleuth*. Below them, on the bottom of Barmet Bay, lay a boat. It was impossible from the surface to identify it as Chet's. Hopefully Frank dived into the water. Half a minute later he reappeared, reporting that it was indeed the *Bloodhound*, but that he had not found the lost key.

After talking the matter over, they proceeded to map out a plan for the search. It was decided that Frank would hunt around the bow of the sunken dory, while Joe would take the stern section.

"Then we'll try midships and the engine," Frank suggested.

The boys took turns. Their first attempts brought no results, and Frank's search of the middle part of the *Bloodhound* did not yield the key, either. They knew that if it had fallen into the shifting sand there would be no chance of finding it. The area around the engine was their last hope.

Joe shot down through the water and grasped the flywheel of the dory's motor. Feeling around quickly with his free hand, he came upon something wedged tightly between the engine and a crossbeam. Pulling it out, he swam quickly to the surface.

"I found it!" Joe yelled jubilantly, and handed the key to Frank.

Joe wanted to go immediately to the Mead house to try it, but his brother reminded him that Chief Collig did not want them to enter the place without a police escort.

"I'd like to take a really good look at this old boat while we're here, anyway," Frank said. "Maybe we can find some identification and get Chet's money back."

"Good idea," Joe agreed. "You swim along one side, and I'll take the other. Suppose I go first."

Joe found nothing, so Frank went over. A few seconds later he came to the surface.

"A mark is carved on the gunwale," he said excitedly. "It looks exactly like that strange Y we saw on John Mead's ring!"

Joe was over the side in a flash to look at the carving himself. He came up, climbed into the *Sleuth,* and started the motor.

"Let's go tell Chet about this," he urged as they raced along. "Maybe it'll help us to find that guy."

Reaching the boathouse, they scrambled into their clothes and drove home. Joe went immediately to the telephone and called Chet to ask him if he had heard from the former owner of the *Bloodhound*. Their friend ruefully admitted that he had not.

"I'm afraid I really got gypped," he said woefully.

"Well, we've picked up a clue for you," Joe said, trying to cheer him up. He told about the odd mark on the dory and the fact that it seemed to be the same as the Y symbol on John Mead's ring. Chet was amazed, but could figure no connection. His description of the boat seller certainly did not fit the man who had nearly crashed into the Hardys on the road.

"Maybe they both belong to some secret society and the Y is their insigne," he suggested.

"Possibly," Joe agreed.

He had hardly hung up the telephone when it started to ring. It was a long-distance call from Mr. Hardy. The detective said he would not be home that night; he was following a new lead on the television thefts.

"How are you making out?" he asked.

Joe related the day's events, admitting that, up to the moment, the clues they had run down had brought no results. His father took a different view, however, saying the elimination of false clues was a battle half won.

"Don't be discouraged, son," he advised. "And visit the Mead house again. I'm certain that if you keep trying you'll find a keyhole somewhere."

Encouraged by the advice, the boys told Mrs. Hardy their plans and drove to police headquarters. Chief Collig was just coming down the front steps as they pulled up.

"Have you solved the Mead mystery?" he asked, walking over to their car.

"Wish we had," Frank responded. "That is why we're here. We'd like to go there again."

The chief frowned. "I can't spare any of my men right now, Frank, and I'd rather you wouldn't do it alone."

"We'll be all right," Frank assured him. "You know we don't take any unnecessary chances."

"Well, tell you what. Go ahead, but call me when you're finished. If I don't hear from you within a couple of hours, I'll send a squad car."

"Fine. And thanks a lot, Chief."

Frank started the car, and soon the boys pulled into the Mead driveway. Frank concealed the car far behind the house.

"Just in case," he said.

"Suppose we take different doors to work on," Joe suggested. "If you find a way in, yell!"

Frank gave the okay sign, and Joe hurried to

the ornate door which faced the water. He surveyed the uniquely carved design critically. There was a keyhole hidden somewhere in the carving. But where?

Closely inspecting the door, Joe started at the right of the panel, pushing at each ridge of the symmetrical design. His search yielded nothing. He tried the left side, without success.

For half an hour he pushed and pulled, growing more puzzled each minute. Finally he tried combinations pressing with both hands on sections of the raised design. Suddenly his efforts were rewarded. Two pieces of molding moved. *A keyhole!*

"Frank!" he called elatedly. "I've found one!"

The tall, dark-haired boy came running. "Great!" he said. "Here, try the key!"

Joe did. A look of disappointment spread over his face. It did not fit.

"Well," he decided, "I suppose it belongs to another door. Come on!"

They walked to the massive front door which Frank had worked on, and once more went over the intricate design. The upper and lower halves were outlined with a wide border, each containing an inset. At first glance the top inset seemed to depict a huge turtle.

Frank, standing at a little distance, suddenly had an idea. "Say, Joe, that turtle's legs look almost like the strange Y symbol!"

Joe stepped back a few yards. "You're right! The two front feet and the right hind one do form a Y, sort of. Wonder if there's an answer here."

Frank pressed his palm against the arched back of the turtle. Suddenly the reptile's right hind foot moved to the side, revealing a large keyhole.

"Look!" he said excitedly, taking the key from Joe and inserting it. "Success!"

Holding his breath, Frank turned the key. There was a clicking sound and the door swung inward on hidden, noiseless hinges.

"Here goes!" Frank whispered as he pocketed the key and stepped over the threshold.

CHAPTER VII

The Mysterious Mansion

WITH a similar thrill of discovery, Joe followed Frank into the dark Mead mansion.

When their eyes became accustomed to the dimness of the shuttered house, the boys gazed around. They were in a large, carpeted entrance hall. The walls were solidly paneled in carved wood, and the Hardys' flashlights revealed that the inside of the front door had the identical turtle design as the outside.

Slowly they went from room to room, peering through the open doorways. Library, living room, dining room—all were tastefully decorated. But the house smelled musty and the furniture was draped with dust sheets, producing a gloomy effect.

"This place hasn't been lived in for a long time," Joe said. "If Mead—or whoever that man on the road was—stayed here, it must have been in the garage!"

"Who *was* that guy, anyhow?" Frank speculated. "Now that we know the key he had fits this house, it makes things more complicated than ever."

Joe agreed. Idly he touched an electric switch on the wall. The dining room suddenly was filled with light. Both boys jumped. "The electricity is on!" Joe said in surprise.

"But why would the power company leave it on in a house that's been closed for five years?" Frank said slowly.

The boys did not speculate further about this, however, because their attention was drawn to the doors and windows. As on the exterior, there was not a sign of hardware on any of them. Locks, latches, bolts, hinges—all must have been ingeniously hidden.

"Let's check out the rest of the place," Joe suggested, snapping off the light switch.

Frank was intrigued by the library with its huge fireplace and hundreds of books. Since he wanted to pause and look at them, Joe said he would go upstairs alone.

"*Locks and Keys* by John Mead," Frank read aloud, noting a handsomely bound volume on a shelf. He removed the dust cover from a reading lamp, switched it on, and sat down in an armchair to glance through the pages.

Instantly his eyes focused on a picture of the author in the front of the book. He did not look at all like the man the boys had encountered! He was elderly, with white hair and a mustache.

"Obviously the deceased owner of this house," Frank decided. He noted that there was no chapter which told how to install concealed hardware.

There was, however, much in the book on the history of locks and keys, and soon Frank became completely absorbed in the subject.

He learned that in Biblical times keys were made of wood and were so heavy that they had to be carried over one's shoulder; that later the makers of metal keys received the name of *locksmith* because actually they were *blacksmiths* who forged keys; and that the invention of burglar-proof locks was barely a hundred years old.

Presently Frank was interrupted by a distant voice saying, "We'd better go now."

"All right, Joe. Just a minute," he replied. But the minute had dragged into five when suddenly the lamp's bulb went out.

Frank got up and hurried into the hall. He clicked on the switch, but this time the lights did not flash on.

"That's funny," he thought. "The main fuse must have blown. Hey, Joe!" he shouted up the dark stairway. "Joe!"

There was no reply.

"Maybe he went outside," Frank said to himself.

Playing his flashlight over the carved design on the inside of the front door, he pressed the turtle's body. At once the door swung inward, and he walked out.

Joe was not around the house, so Frank hurried to the convertible. But he was not there, either. After looking over the grounds, going as far as the waterfront, Frank decided that his brother still was in the mansion.

Meanwhile, Joe was having his own difficulties. He had paused in a den to look at some hunting trophies which hung on the walls. Switching on a lamp, he gazed in admiration at several fine specimens. In moving about, he accidentally closed the door leading into the hall. It locked!

"Now that was stupid of me," he muttered, looking for the combination to open it.

Suddenly the lamp went out. To his chagrin, Joe realized that he had left his flashlight on a table in the downstairs hall. And now he could not see the design on the door well enough to work on it.

He hurried to one of the shuttered windows, through which rays of sunshine filtered, and lifted the sash. "Well, that's a break," he thought.

Getting the shutters open was another matter. Though no fastener was visible, they were locked. Joe ran his fingers over the surface hunting for a secret spring, but found none. Next he took a penknife from his pocket and inserted one of its blades in the crack between the two shutters. Suddenly there was a click, and they opened.

Looking out, he saw his brother standing below. "Hey, Frank!" he yelled.

The older boy looked up in amazement. "So that's where you are! I've been looking all over for you. Come on down. We'd better go now, or the chief will send a car for us."

Joe leaned from the window and surveyed the wall of the mansion. There was no possible way for him to climb to the ground, and the drop was too far to be made safely.

"I can't get out," he announced.

"What?"

"The door to this room is locked," Joe explained, "and I left my flashlight downstairs. Come on up and see if you can open it from outside."

"Okay."

Frank reentered the house and quickly found the room where Joe was imprisoned. He played his flashlight over the door panels, scrutinizing every detail of the ornate floral design.

"How'd you get in?" he called out.

"It was open," Joe replied.

Frank pushed and pulled at each flower of the pattern. Suddenly one of the blooms slid aside, revealing a small latch. Frank lifted it with a finger and the door swung inward.

"Whew! I'm glad to get out of here," Joe said in relief. "What happened to the lights?"

"I don't know. A fuse must have blown."

As Joe retrieved his flashlight and followed Frank from the house, he asked him what he had found in the library.

"Some excellent books on locks and keys," Frank replied. "One by John Mead. I'll tell you about it as we drive home."

Joe listened to his brother attentively, and made no comment until Frank mentioned that he was sorry to have been interrupted in his reading.

"Who interrupted you?" Joe asked.

"You!"

"What do you mean?"

"You said we'd better go."

"I never said that!"

"Someone did!" Frank said, looking surprised. "I distinctly heard a voice call out, 'We'd better go now.'"

"Good grief!" Joe ran his fingers through his hair. "There must have been two other persons in the house!"

"Two or even more," Frank added dryly.

"Which means they have a key, too, and know how to use it!"

"I wonder if they knew we were there," Frank

said. "We hid the car, and unless they saw us without our noticing them . . ."

"We just can't be sure," Joe muttered. "They must have switched off the power, too."

"It could have been the guy who called himself John Mead," Frank went on. "And someone else, of course."

"Why didn't we see their car?" Joe wondered.

"They could have arrived after us and left before we did."

Joe sighed. "More problems."

Frank drove on, deep in thought. As they approached an intersection, the traffic light changed and he jammed on the brakes. Neither of the boys spoke as they waited for the green signal.

Suddenly Joe asked, "Frank, do you hear what I hear?"

"It hums!" Frank said. "Maybe this is the singing light Dr. Gardner was talking about!"

"Look, why don't we start out at once and drive ten minutes in various directions? Maybe we'll find Lenny Stryker!"

"Good idea. But let's call Chief Collig first and tell him we're out of the Mead house."

Frank parked in front of a phone booth not far from the humming traffic light and soon had the chief on the line. He reported everything they had experienced and told him about their latest clue.

Chief Collig had no news concerning Lenny and wished the boys luck in their search.

When Frank returned to the car, he said, "We can't go east because of the bay. And we should save the direction toward town until last. We can look around there after dinner."

"Right. Let's go west first and see what's down this road."

In exactly ten minutes the boys stopped in front of an open pasture in a farming section.

"No hideout here," Joe said, disappointed.

Frank drove back to the singing light and then headed north. Five minutes later they passed the Mead property and gazed intently into the grounds. There was no sign of anyone. In another five minutes they reached a tiny village which consisted of a general store, a garage, a church, and a few homes. Frank parked the car.

"Peaceful-looking place," he remarked. "I wonder if we'll find a clue here."

They decided to investigate the garage first. Inside the barnlike building, a youth in overalls was washing a car.

"Where's your boss?" Joe spoke up.

"Dunno."

While Joe questioned the mechanic about the town's residents and newcomers, in an effort to find a lead about Lenny and the gang of thieves, Frank wandered into the small office adjoining the garage.

As he peered around, he noticed a sheet of paper lying on the desk. It was crinkled, as if from dampness, and a corner was torn off. Frank picked it up. It contained a typed list of various appliance and television dealers in the area. Two stores in Bayport and a warehouse in Southport had an X mark after the names.

Frank gasped. Those were the places that had been robbed within the last two weeks!

CHAPTER VIII

Tricked!

As Frank stared at the list in amazement, the mechanic walked into the office. He noticed the boy's strange look and the sheet of paper in his hand.

"What's the matter?" he asked. "You're looking at that as if it were a check for a million dollars!"

Frank said nothing, and the mechanic went on, "I found it outside in the tall grass. Thought it might belong to the boss. He didn't want it, though."

On a sudden hunch Frank asked him if he had changed the tire for Mr. Mead the previous morning.

"Dunno. I change a lot of tires."

"The one I mean was in the front," Frank added, trying to jog the young man's memory.

"Don't remember." With that the mechanic left the office again, just as Joe entered.

Frank drew his brother aside and reminded

him of two significant facts: The garage was only a five-minute drive from the Mead home, and the man who had used John Mead's name had told them he had his tire changed by a boy! This was surely the same place, Frank reasoned. Could Mead have dropped the list here? Was he one of the television thieves?

Just then a middle-aged man in overalls came in. A label on his breast pocket bore the name Carl Bilks. "Can I help you?" he asked.

Frank's mind whirled with new and unanswered questions. Was Bilks in league with the thieves? If so, he would certainly be suspicious if Frank asked him about the list.

"Oh—ah—I was trying to find out if you changed a tire for a friend of mine yesterday," Frank said.

"You'll have to ask the kid outside," Bilks replied. "He takes care of that."

"I did. He can't remember."

"Why do you want to know? Is anything wrong?"

"Yes. The wheel came off."

"Now look here," Bilks replied heatedly, "I'm sure it wasn't done in this garage. My assistant is a trained and competent mechanic. You must have the wrong place, mister!"

"Probably." Frank nodded and changed the subject. "I found this on the floor." He handed the garage owner the list.

Bilks glanced at it. "Oh, I don't need that. The kid found it outside and thought it belonged to me, but I don't have any idea what it is." He took the sheet and tossed it into the wastebasket.

"Well, we'll be running along," said Frank. "Good-by, Mr. Bilks." With that the boys left quickly.

On the way back to Bayport they discussed the new turn of events.

"You think Bilks and his mechanic are telling the truth about that list?" Joe asked.

"I have a hunch they are. It looked as if it had been wet—it might very well have been lying in the grass for a while. But still, it's not conclusive proof that everyone at the garage is on the level. I memorized the list and we'll ask Chief Collig to give us a rundown on Bilks."

As they passed the humming traffic signal, Joe checked the time again. They went in a southerly direction, and ten minutes later Frank was driving through a residential section of town.

"Okay, let's remember this spot and come back after dinner," Frank suggested.

"Right."

At home they were greeted by Aunt Gertrude. "Well, you just about made it," she said. "A few more minutes and everything would have been cold!"

"Don't you know, Aunty, our timing is always perfect!" Joe quipped.

"Don't brag," his aunt retorted. "Sit down instead."

The boys enjoyed a hearty meal of roast chicken, potatoes, and asparagus. While eating, they related the day's events. Then Frank announced that they were going out to do a little more sleuthing after dinner.

"I declare," Aunt Gertrude said, sniffing. "I don't know what's happening to this generation. Never get proper sleep. They'll all be nervous wrecks before they're thirty."

Concealing their amusement, the boys hurried from the house. Upon reaching the residential section ten minutes south of the second humming traffic light, they parked and walked through the area. After spending half an hour making inquiries, they were convinced that this was not where Dr. Gardner had been taken.

"Why don't we run out to Chet's?" Joe suggested. "Maybe he knows something new."

"Good idea," Frank agreed. "Especially since Iola might be there."

"Okay, okay," Joe said, grinning. "Cut it out." He was very fond of Chet's sister Iola, who was his frequent date.

When the Hardys reached the Morton farm, Chet's mother and sister came out to the front porch and greeted them excitedly.

"Chet's been trying to call you," Mrs. Morton

said with a smile, "but you weren't home. Finally he couldn't wait any longer and left."

"What's up?" Joe asked, looking puzzled.

"I don't know," replied dark-haired, slim Iola. "He was kind of mysterious about the whole thing."

"Yes, and rather agitated," Mrs. Morton added. "He asked me to continue trying to contact you, and if I did, to tell you to meet him at 47 Parker Street."

The Hardys had never heard of that street, and all Mrs. Morton could add was that Chet had told her he was to meet a man on some special business.

"We'd better get going, Joe," Frank urged.

They bid the Mortons good-by and drove off quickly, their thoughts whirling. Had Chet found the trail of the man who had sold him the battered dory? Or had he somehow picked up a clue to the whereabouts of Lenny Stryker or the television thieves?

When they located Parker Street, they saw that it led to Bayport's waterfront. A street lamp revealed number 47 as an old dilapidated house.

"You think this is the place Chet meant?" Frank asked, surveying the closed windows and drawn shades.

"Sure seems funny," Joe admitted. "I don't like it. Certainly looks deserted."

Just then a short, stocky man walked slowly up the alleyway from the back of the house.

"Hey," Frank whispered, nudging his brother, "I'll bet he's the guy who sold Chet the boat!"

"Could be," Joe agreed in a low voice. "He fits the description."

The boys stepped up to the man just as he reached the sidewalk. Joe said he was looking for a friend and wondered if the stranger had seen him. The man shook his head.

"Haven't seen anybody. Been too busy." He started up the street.

"We were to meet him here," Frank put in, looking intently at the man. "Are you sure he didn't come to this house?"

The man returned his gaze levelly, then countered by asking why they were meeting their friend at this place.

Frank decided impulsively that a straightforward answer was best. He replied that they were trying to find the person who had sold Chet Morton the dory.

"And we think you're that person!" Joe added.

The Hardys expected the man to deny the accusation, but to their surprise he burst into laughter. "Oh, so that's it," he said. "Sure, I sold your pal a boat. And I've been tryin' ever since to find him. I want to buy it back."

"You—you want to get it back?" Frank cried in amazement.

The stocky man seemed to be surprised by the boy's reaction. "What's the matter with that?" he said. "It belonged to my brother, and I thought he wanted to get rid of it. Turns out he'd like to keep it after all. In fact I'll pay your buddy extra to get it back. Where can I find him?"

Frank's suspicions were aroused now. He was sure Chet had already given his name and address to the man. "We'll tell him your message when we see him. Where can he get in touch with you?"

"Come on inside and I'll get you one of my cards," the man said.

Frank and Joe looked at each other. Was this a trap? And where was Chet? They decided to be on guard.

Slowly they followed the man up the front porch of number 47 and into the hallway. He snapped on a ceiling light, apologizing for the bleak appearance of the house. His furniture, he said, consisted at the moment only of the pieces in his office at the rear. Keeping alert for anything unusual, Frank and Joe walked with him to the end of the hall and waited as he unlocked a door.

He stepped inside and reached for the light switch. The boys followed as a lamp flicked on. The next moment the stranger whirled about, grabbed Joe by the shoulders, and thrust him against Frank.

As the Hardys crashed to the floor, their assailant leaped out of the room, slammed the door, and locked it from the outside.

They heard him hastily retreating up the hallway. Then the light went out. Obviously he had turned off the main fuse on his way out. The front door slammed shut and there was nothing but silence for a moment.

In the darkness Frank sat up. "Are you all right, Joe?"

"Yes. And you?"

"I'm okay. But that guy sure walloped us."

Suddenly a loud groan came from somewhere in the pitch-black room.

Frank got up and felt around for his flashlight, which had dropped from his pocket. He located it and snapped it on. Behind the desk lay a figure, bound and gagged.

The Hardys hastened to the captive and knelt down, shining the light on his face. *Chet Morton!*

CHAPTER IX

Found and Lost

QUICKLY Frank and Joe pulled the handkerchief from Chet's mouth, untied the cords that bound his wrists and ankles, and rubbed them vigorously. Chet soon regained full consciousness.

"Wh-where am I?" he gasped. Then, recognizing the Hardys, he added, "Thank goodness you came."

"Tell us what happened!" Joe exclaimed.

Frank suggested they leave the house right away. At any instant the stocky stranger might return with reinforcements.

There was a telephone on the desk. Joe picked it up, but the line was dead. "That figures," he commented.

Glancing around, the boys observed that the desk and a small table with two chairs were the only pieces of furniture in the room. One window was high up. Apparently its lock was rusted shut.

The other exit from the room was through the wooden door to the hall.

They threw their weight against it and after several attempts the upper half gave way. Another heave against the door made an opening large enough for them to crawl through. Seconds later they left the house.

The street was quiet and no one was in sight.

"Where's your car?" Frank asked Chet.

"I parked around the corner."

"No wonder we didn't see it," Joe said. "We were wondering if we had the right address."

The boys drove to the Morton farm. Frank and Joe went inside with their chum and Mrs. Morton served milk and apple pie.

"Okay, Chet, let's have your story from the beginning," Frank urged when Mrs. Morton had left the room.

Chet told them he had received a mysterious telephone call earlier that evening. He was told to go immediately to 47 Parker Street to see about the dory he had bought.

"I thought there was a chance I'd get my money back," he explained, "so I drove over there. When I arrived, the guy who sold me the boat said he wanted it back. At first I didn't let him know it was at the bottom of the bay."

"What did you tell him?" Joe asked.

"That I wanted to keep it. He glared at me and said I certainly *was* going to sell it back to him. I was hoping you would come any moment, so I kept putting him off. He got madder by the minute."

"I wonder why he wants that old tub back," Joe said. "The story about his brother sounds phony."

"I don't know." Chet shrugged. "But when I finally told him it had sunk, boy did he rave! I tried to get out but he locked the front door. He made me describe the place where it had gone under—and then the next thing I knew, he gave me a terrific blast on the head. I blacked out."

Before they left, the Hardys promised their friend they would continue looking for the stranger. It would be easier now that they had met him face to face.

"We have something to pay him back for, too," Joe said grimly. "We don't like to be shoved around."

After reporting the episode to the police, the boys headed for home. Mrs. Hardy and Aunt Gertrude had already retired when they reached their house. They were just about to go to bed when they heard their father's key in the front door.

"Let's talk to him," Joe urged Frank, and ran down the stairs. "Hello, Dad. How did you make out?" he asked eagerly.

Mr. Hardy said he was a bit discouraged as far as the television burglaries were concerned. He was working on a new angle involving finger-prints.

The three went to his study, where Frank and Joe related their experiences that day. It took some time to tell about the humming traffic light; the strange happenings at the Mead mansion; the list at Bilks' garage and the adventures at 47 Parker Street.

When they finished, Mr. Hardy was thoughtful. "I think we can assume your assailant locked you all in to make sure you wouldn't try to follow him."

He tapped the desk with a pencil. "The fact that he made Chet describe the spot where the dory went down indicates that he certainly wants it back badly. I'm inclined to think that someone else wants that boat, and it's not his brother."

"The boat itself certainly can't have any value," Frank mused.

"Right. There must be more involved."

Frank thought the strange Y carved on the gunwale might be a clue, and Joe reminded him about the locked box in the bow.

Their father suggested raising the boat and examining it thoroughly. "I think the Bayport Salvage Company would do the job," he said. "Go over there tomorrow and ask for Mr. Redfield."

At breakfast the next morning Mr. Hardy announced he had to see Chief Collig at headquarters about the television burglaries.

"Dad," Frank said, looking disappointed, "we were hoping you'd come to the Mead place with us! Maybe you'll spot something important that we overlooked."

"Okay. But let's do it right away. I have a couple of important things to do later."

The three set off immediately after they had eaten. Frank and Joe followed their father's car in the convertible. When they arrived at the mysterious mansion, it looked deserted. They parked their cars in the back so they would not be seen by any visitor. Mr. Hardy walked around the grounds before entering the house. He found no one on the premises.

When Frank opened the front door, Mr. Hardy was fascinated by the concealed hardware. "You're to be congratulated," he praised the boys. "These locks are quite a puzzle."

Joe felt for the wall switch and clicked it, but no light came on.

"Current's still off," he remarked.

The boys showed their father through the house, using their flashlights when necessary. They admired their father's careful search, even though it netted no clues to the man who called himself John Mead.

Presently the three returned to their cars.

"I'm off to see Chief Collig," Mr. Hardy said. "Are you going straight to Bayport Salvage?"

"Yes," Joe replied. "Maybe they can look for Chet's boat today."

The detective wished them luck and drove away.

A few minutes later Frank and Joe reached the salvage company. When they entered the front office, a man working on some ledgers looked up.

"Mr. Redfield?" Frank inquired.

"Yes. May I help you?"

Frank stated their business. As he described the sunken dory, Mr. Redfield looked startled. "What's going on here?" he asked. "Do you own that boat?"

"No," Joe replied. "It belongs to a friend."

"Oh, well, that makes sense, then. Your friend has already gone out on one of our boats to look for it."

"Our friend?" Frank was perplexed. "What did he look like?"

"Stocky and dark. Said he was the owner and he's out in the bay right now!"

The Hardys turned to each other. "That isn't Chet!" Frank cried. "That's the guy who tricked us!"

"Come on," Joe urged. "Let's get the *Sleuth* and go after him!"

They quickly explained the situation to Mr. Redfield, then raced outside, hopped into their car, and not long afterward parked near the boat-house where they kept the *Sleuth*.

Joe had the engine going in no time, and sped out into Barmet Bay. He headed for the spot where Chet's dory had sunk. No salvage boat was in sight. To the boys' dismay, they could see no sign of the *Bloodhound*, though they circled round and round the vicinity, peering down through the water.

"They must have raised it!" Frank concluded.

"Now what'll we do?" Joe asked in disgust.

"Let's go back to the salvage company."

Joe headed the *Sleuth* in that direction. They had gone only a mile when they spied the salvage boat ahead. Hoping that Chet's dory was aboard, and that they could nab the man who had ordered it raised, they drew up alongside and hailed the captain. He came to the rail.

"What did you say?" he called down.

Frank repeated his question.

"Yes, I raised a sunken dory, but I haven't got 'er aboard," the man replied.

"Where is it?"

"I put 'er down on the beach where the fellow told me to."

"But he didn't own it!"

"What?" The captain was astounded upon hearing the story. He told the Hardys where he had left the *Bloodhound*.

The boys thanked him and Joe swung the *Sleuth* toward the north shore of the bay. The bow cut clearly through the water, churning a white wake as it picked up speed.

"We're sure running into some bad luck," Joe said, gripping the wheel.

"Maybe we can still capture the guy and get the dory, too," Frank countered.

There was no doubt in his mind that the man who retrieved it was the same who had sold it to Chet and had trapped the three boys in the room at 47 Parker Street.

"Meanwhile, the guy probably took what he wanted out of the locked box and skipped," Joe went on.

"Well, let's go see."

When they reached the spot indicated by the salvage captain, there was no sign of the dory. Frank and Joe jumped into the shallow water and pulled the *Sleuth* up on the sand.

Close scrutiny led them to drag marks some distance away. They followed the track, obviously made by a keel. But to their disappointment, it ended at the roadside. Chet's *Bloodhound* was not in sight!

"Evidently a truck was waiting and carried it away," Joe concluded.

"I have an idea!" Frank said. "I'll bet that dory came from the Mead place and has been taken back there!"

"You mean because of the strange Y symbol?"

"Right. What do you think?"

"It's certainly worth a try. Let's go!"

Joe stepped into the *Sleuth* and Frank pushed

"Where is the dory?" Frank called

it out into the bay. Soon it was skimming across the water, its motor churning. When they reached the Mead property, Frank tied up to the dock. There was no sign of anyone. The boathouse was tightly locked, and Chet's dory was not in sight.

Joe took out a pair of swim trunks from a compartment.

"What are you going to do?" Frank asked.

"See if I can swim under the boathouse door." Joe quickly changed, then cut the water in a clean dive and disappeared.

Frank waited eagerly. All was quiet. In a minute he called out, "Joe, can you hear me?"

The only sound was the water lapping against the *Sleuth*. There was no sound from the boathouse!

CHAPTER X

The Intruder

WHAT had happened to Joe? Several possibilities raced through Frank's mind. Had his head butted into a submerged piling? Did he have a stomach cramp?

"Joe! Joe!" Frank called out again. No reply. He kicked off his shoes and was about to dive after his brother when he heard a whistling-spluttering noise from inside the boathouse. Joe had popped to the surface and let out a chestful of pent-up air. Then he called out:

"Frank! I'm okay. Got tangled up in a piece of old cable."

"Oh boy! You had me scared for a minute."

"Sorry about that." A few seconds passed, then Joe reported, "The dory's not here. But I'll look around a bit more."

"Good idea." Frank waited, hoping no one would appear to ask what they were doing there.

Presently Joe returned and climbed aboard the *Sleuth*. As he dried himself and put on his clothes, Frank asked him what he had seen.

Joe related that there was no boat of any kind inside the building. He had, however, spotted a valuable piece of evidence.

"There was an old oar on a rack," he said. "That same funny Y was carved on it!"

"Are you sure?"

"Positive. I looked at it twice."

"No question now that the dory belongs to this place," Frank commented.

"Right. And I saw something else of interest," Joe went on. "There's a generator in the boathouse. Probably supplies auxiliary power to the mansion."

"Then that explains the lights," Frank declared. "Someone's been tampering with the generator, turning the current on and off."

"Right again," said Joe. "You know, I still suspect that the dory will be brought here. What say we come back later and check again?"

"Okay. But we ought to tell Chet what happened. Maybe he'd like to come along."

"Yes. Let's go over to the Mortons around lunch time," Joe suggested with a grin. "Turn the tables on Chet. Aunt Gertrude says he eats us out of house and home."

Frank chuckled. "Great idea. Mrs. Morton is about the best cook in the world."

When the boys reached home they told their mother where they were going. But they could not get out of the house without Aunt Gertrude remarking about it.

"Gallivanting again!" she said sternly. "Home the last thing at night and out first thing in the morning. Now you've been in this house just about five minutes, and already you're off again!"

"Oh," said Joe, a twinkle in his eye, "this is strictly business, Aunty. We're working on a case for Chet."

Before Miss Hardy could think of an answer, the boys had disappeared through the doorway. They got into their convertible and headed for the Morton farm. As Joe had predicted, the midday meal was about to be served.

Chet's sister Iola was glad to see them, especially Joe. She told Frank to go into the living room. "Surprise!" she said with a broad smile.

Frank found Callie Shaw there, watching television. The brown-eyed, vivacious girl was his favorite date.

"Oh, hi, Frank!" Callie said, beaming. "I had a hunch you might be coming."

"You did?"

"A little bird was on the news just a minute ago. He said so!"

Frank laughed. "No kidding. Is that why you decided to stay for lunch?"

Callie blushed. She got even with him when Mrs. Morton came in.

"Frank and Joe have eaten already and won't join us for lunch," she said with a wink.

"I'm so sorry," Mrs. Morton said, taking her cue from Callie. "We're having barbecued spare-ribs and biscuits."

Then, seeing Frank's hungry expression, she laughed good-naturedly and said she would set two more places at the table at once, and asked Frank to call Chet. "He's out spraying the apple trees."

Frank went to find his friend, who was de-lighted to be relieved of his job, and started for the house.

"Wait a minute," Frank said. "I have some-thing to tell you."

He related how the dory had been salvaged. Chet's eyes nearly popped from their sockets; then he shook his head sadly and groaned. "Now what am I going to do?"

He brightened, however, when Frank told him that he and Joe were going back to the Mead house later to see if the *Bloodhound* had been brought there.

Chet was sorry not to be able to go along be-cause of his afternoon chores at the farm, but he expressed confidence in his friends' ability to solve his problem. As the two walked toward the house, he asked Frank not to mention anything to his folks about the boat.

During lunch the young people made plans for a triple date to the movies that evening. Chet called his girl, Helen Osborne, and invited her to the show. Soon after dessert the Hardys left the house.

They were eager to clear up the mystery of Chet's dory. Since they planned to be at the movies that evening, they decided to return at once to the Mead mansion.

When they arrived at the estate, they concealed their car in a tangle of trees. Then they looked for evidence of recent visitors. There were no footprints or automobile tracks near the boathouse.

"Probably the dory hasn't been brought here yet," Joe deduced.

"Why don't we have another look around the place as long as we're here?" Frank suggested. He opened the front door and clicked on the light in the hall. Nothing happened.

"Whoever turns on the generator isn't here now, that's for sure," he remarked. "Let's do a little investigating in the cellar and try to find where the line comes in."

Frank snapped on his flashlight and led the way below. For the next few minutes they hunted in vain for any sign of a fuse box.

"Maybe old Mr. Mead concealed it as he did the locks and latches," said Frank, almost slipping on the damp floor as he reached up on a wall shelf. There was no sign of the incoming power line.

Joe noticed a wooden panel on the wall. "Hey, Frank," he said, "have a look at this!"

Frank came over and studied it carefully. He placed his hands on the bottom of the panel and pushed. It slid open!

"Fuses!" he cried, beaming his flashlight inside.

"I wonder why the cover is off," Joe remarked. "Usually fuse boxes have a metal cover."

"I don't know," Frank replied. He reached up and touched one of the oblong handles. The basement was flooded with light. At the same instant Frank received an electrical shock and fell to the floor unconscious!

Joe leaped to his brother's side and felt for his pulse. The beat was weak but steady.

"Thank goodness he's alive!" he murmured, and quickly administered first aid. In a few moments Frank opened his eyes, wondering what had happened.

Joe told him and suggested they go upstairs where Frank could lie down on a sofa.

When they reached the kitchen, Frank was so weak he sat down in a chair. He told Joe to look around the house alone while he rested. The younger boy nodded and started off.

Going from room to room, he tried the lights. In some places they flashed on, in others they did not.

Joe was just about to step into the library, which was dark, when he heard a loud groan.

"Frank!" he thought, conscience-stricken, and rushed back to the kitchen.

His brother still sat in the chair and was deadly white. He admitted feeling awful. Joe insisted they leave at once, and helped Frank to the car.

By the time they reached home Frank felt much better. "I'm made of pretty tough stuff," he said with a faint grin.

"You were lucky!" Joe agreed. "If the current had been more powerful you—" He broke off. "Hold it," he warned as he pulled open the kitchen screen door. "Something's the matter here!"

"What do you mean?" Frank asked.

The words were hardly out of his mouth when he, too, became aware of women's loud voices in the front hall. Aunt Gertrude seemed to be consoling someone. A moment later the boys recognized the other speaker as Mrs. Stryker.

"My son's honest and I want him back!" she cried out. "Nobody seems to be doing anything for me!"

"You have no right to talk about my brother and my nephews that way!" Miss Hardy replied with spirit. "They're the best detectives in this state; in fact, the best in the whole United States!"

Despite the seriousness of the situation, Frank and Joe looked at each other and grinned. This was high praise from their aunt. High praise which she would not have voiced had she known they were listening.

Winking at Frank, Joe turned around and slammed the kitchen door. Then, with a "Hello, anybody home?" he stalked into the front hall.

Frank followed. "Have you had any word from Lenny?" he asked Mrs. Stryker.

The woman shook her head, remarking that she had heard from no one. "Those racketeers have things fixed so he can't let me know where he is," she said sadly. Then she added, "I thought you and your father were working on his case for me. But all I get are promises!"

"Try not to worry," urged Frank. "I have a hunch Lenny will be coming home soon."

"You have?" Mrs. Stryker asked eagerly. "Oh, you must know something you're not telling me!"

The Hardys had to admit that they really were no closer to the solution of the mystery, but they were hopeful that clues they had gathered would lead them to the gang.

"Clues, clues, you told me that before!" Mrs. Stryker said.

"We'll do everything we can," Joe assured her.

After she had left, the boys held a conference. Aunt Gertrude insisted upon being present, and advised her nephews that the police should track down the criminals, not they.

"Lenny Stryker probably did some shooting himself," she declared.

"We certainly won't let anybody who should be in jail go free," Frank stated. "But—"

The telephone rang and the boys hurried into the hall. Joe answered it. It was his father. He listened intently as Joe related the day's happenings, ending with Frank's electrical shock. Mr. Hardy warned Joe to be very careful, saying they most likely were on the trail of some illegal operation.

"Pass that along to Frank," he ordered. "Now I'll tell you my plans."

He explained that there were only two major appliance warehouses in the close vicinity which had not been burglarized.

"They were both on the list you saw at Bilks' garage. We have a hunch they will be robbed, even though the thieves must know they will be extra well guarded. I can't give you the details over the phone," he went on, "but I won't be home tonight. Tell Mother not to worry. See you all in the morning."

Joe repeated the conversation to his brother. They felt certain that their father was going to lie in wait inside one of the warehouses.

The boys were still discussing their father's telephone call when Mrs. Hardy came home, and they gave her his message. Aunt Gertrude had dinner ready, and as usual she insisted they all sit down at once to eat.

"One of your old school friends is coming over this evening, Laura," she announced presently.

"Who's that?" asked Mrs. Hardy.

"Frank, eat more slowly," Aunt Gertrude ordered. "Laura, these boys certainly are going to ruin their digestion if they stuff themselves like this."

"But, Aunty, we've just started," Frank pointed out.

"That makes no difference. I know by the way you two are setting out you plan to eat enough for four people. Oh, yes," she added, "Martha Johnson is coming to call."

"I'm so glad," said Mrs. Hardy. Then, turning to her sons, she explained that Miss Johnson was a high school friend. "She became a nurse and moved to the West Coast. She comes back every so often, but I haven't seen her for several years."

Aunt Gertrude said Miss Johnson was on a short visit in Bayport, and had telephoned to see if the Hardys were at home. The boys' mother was eagerly looking forward to seeing her friend. Shortly after dinner the woman arrived.

Frank and Joe talked with Miss Johnson for a while, then excused themselves to keep their movie date with Chet and the girls.

After they had left, the three women settled

themselves in the living room for a long talk. Presently the conversation became so animated and full of laughter that they failed to hear the back door open softly and a stealthy figure tiptoe in. The man who entered listened to them for several moments. Then a cunning gleam came into his eyes.

CHAPTER XI

Kidnapped

"PERFECT," the intruder said to himself. "The dame in there is a nurse, eh? That solves our problem just fine."

He moved on upstairs to Mr. Hardy's study. Reaching it, he went directly to the detective's filing cabinet. He took out a small tool and began skillfully to work on the lock. Soon it opened. One by one, he noiselessly pulled out the drawers.

Suddenly his eyes lighted up as he came upon a marked folder. Quickly he removed the papers from it and put them into his pocket.

At the same moment he heard Aunt Gertrude say, "Well, how about some coffee, Martha? I'll go fix it."

The intruder froze on the spot. He waited until Miss Hardy had finished the coffee and taken it into the living room, then silently tiptoed downstairs again.

While the women were chatting gaily, he streaked through the kitchen and a second later had left the house.

Meanwhile, after a pleasant time at the local theater, Frank and Joe dropped off Chet and the girls and started for home. As they neared the house, Frank heaved a sigh.

"I'm so full of ice cream I could burst."

Joe thumped his stomach. "I feel like Chet looks. If— Oh!"

A woman's frantic scream pierced the air. The boys drove toward the spot, but found nobody. A moment later they heard a car roar off a short distance away.

"What do you make of that?" Frank asked.

Joe shook his head. "Sounded like someone was in plenty of trouble. Let's report it to the police."

They pulled into their driveway, parked the convertible in the garage, and entered the house. They had just reached the hall when a shriek came from their father's study.

"Aunt Gertrude!" shouted Frank and dashed upstairs. Joe followed.

They expected to see their relative prostrate, the victim of some kind of attack. To their relief, they found her standing in the center of the room, unharmed.

"What's the matter?" Frank asked.

His aunt was speechless. Finally she was able to stammer, "The filing cabinet!"

The boys gasped as they noticed a slightly opened drawer, and jumped to the same conclusion. *A burglar!*

They checked drawer after drawer. Although not familiar with everything in the cabinet, they soon found the empty folder that had contained the fingerprint records of the television thieves.

"We've been robbed!" exclaimed Frank.

"Mike Batton!" Joe cried out.

Aunt Gertrude demanded an explanation. Joe told her how Ben Whittaker's assistant had been tampering with their back-door lock two days before.

"Batton claimed he was supposed to change it, but we sent him away," Frank said. "Now I believe he must have taken a wax impression, made a key, and came back tonight."

"That means he's tied in with the television thieves!" Joe reasoned.

Suddenly Frank had an idea. "I wonder if the woman's scream had anything to do with the intruder."

"You mean when he left the house he might have frightened her?" Joe asked.

Frank nodded. "The burglar went out the back way. Running from the house like that, he might easily have scared some passer-by."

Frank turned to his aunt. "When did Miss Johnson leave here?"

"A few minutes ago. Why? And what's that about a scream?"

"Didn't *you* hear it?"

"No!"

Frank reported the frantic cry they had heard. Aunt Gertrude had not noticed it, because a moment after the nurse had left she had turned on the television for the late news.

Now Mrs. Hardy appeared in the doorway. She had not heard anything, not even Aunt Gertrude's shriek in the study. When she was told what had happened, she became quite concerned.

"It frightens me to think of a burglar being in the house," she said with a shiver.

"It's positively wicked!" Aunt Gertrude agreed, "If I had seen that fellow I would have—"

Frank interrupted her. "Where is Miss Johnson staying, Mom?"

"At Mrs. Brown's Guest House."

"Did she take a taxi there?"

"No. It's not far and she was going to walk."

Frank went to the telephone and called at once to see if the nurse had returned. Mrs. Brown told him her guest had not come back.

"When she does, will you please have her telephone Mrs. Hardy," the boy requested. "It's important."

Next, the boys notified Chief Collig. They reached him at home, and he promised to start a search at once.

But in spite of the police alert, there was no news of Miss Johnson when the Hardys finally went to bed long after midnight.

In the morning they called Mrs. Brown's Guest House again. The nurse had not returned.

"Oh dear! This is dreadful!" Mrs. Hardy exclaimed. "No telling what has happened to Martha. What can we do?"

Her sons could think of nothing at the moment, but by the time breakfast was over they had arrived at a theory.

"We've assumed Batton was our thief last night and that he's tied in with the TV burglars," Frank began. "We also figure he kidnapped Miss Johnson.

"Now, since Lenny is presumably being held by the same gang," he continued, "isn't it likely Martha Johnson was nabbed to be a nurse for him because of his leg wound?"

"Sure!" Joe agreed. "Batton must have been in the house long enough to overhear who she was, and grabbed her as she left."

"So if we find the secret panel, we'll find both Lenny and Miss Johnson," Frank concluded.

"But where will you begin your search?" Mrs. Hardy asked.

"First we'll go down and talk to Ben Whittaker again," said Frank. "He may have heard from Mike Batton."

"Or perhaps the police can tell us something by now," Joe suggested.

Frank also thought they should go to the Mead estate and dive under the boathouse door to see if Chet's stolen dory had been taken there.

"It sounds like a full morning," said Mrs. Hardy. "Please let Chet's mystery wait and try to find Martha."

"We certainly will, Mother."

Suddenly from the kitchen radio came a news broadcast to which Aunt Gertrude had just tuned.

"—A local item of great interest," stated the announcer, "is about another baffling burglary."

Frank, Joe, and their mother entered the kitchen to listen attentively as the newscaster went on:

"Thieves broke into the Carr Electronics Company last night. Televisions, tubes, and stereo equipment were stolen. The police are mystified. No one was seen entering the place, and Fenton Hardy, a detective on guard duty inside, was found injured. He has been taken to the hospital!"

CHAPTER XII

Fingerprints

THE four beside the kitchen radio were shocked by the news that Mr. Hardy was lying in a hospital, the victim of some desperate criminal. The boys' mother tapped nervously on the table. For once Aunt Gertrude seemed tongue-tied. Joe was the first to find his voice.

"Let's call Chief Collig!" he cried, starting for the telephone.

"Wait a minute!" Frank caught his brother's arm. "I don't believe it *is* Dad!"

He explained that if Mr. Hardy really had been hurt, surely his family would have been notified by this time. Aunt Gertrude, now over her scare, declared, "Well, knowing my brother as I do, I'd say the whole thing is a hoax!"

"What do you mean?" Mrs. Hardy asked.

"I believe it's a clever idea of Fenton's. If he pretends to be injured, and those television thieves think he's in a hospital, they'll be less cautious when they strike again."

"And Dad will trap them!" said Joe. "I'll bet you're right, Aunt Gertrude."

Aunt Gertrude looked pleased. "So I guess we needn't worry any more about Fenton. You boys can get started looking for Martha."

For a few seconds Frank and Joe had forgotten the work they had mapped out for themselves. Now, being reminded, they left the house. Their first stop was police headquarters to see Chief Collig.

To their first question, Collig replied that he had no word from the boys' father. But he verified the assumption that the story of the hospitalized detective was a phony.

"No, nothing on Miss Johnson," he replied to Frank's next query. "We've got half a dozen of our best men out looking, though."

Frank and Joe decided it was now imperative that they relate Mrs. Stryker's story of the secret panel. They told the chief their suspicions about the television thieves.

"Well, that would explain why Miss Johnson was kidnapped," Collig remarked. "With you two, your father, and most of the police in this country tracking that gang, we should crack this case soon."

"I sure hope so," Joe replied.

Then, in answer to a query from Frank, the

chief told the boys he had given orders for a constant surveillance of the house at 47 Parker Street.

"Not a soul has gone in or out since," he reported.

"Would you mind if we go over there now and look around inside?" Frank asked. "I'm sure the Parker Street house is connected with the other mysteries."

"It's all right with me. So far as I know, the place is vacant."

"Where can we get a key?" Joe asked. "Or is it open?"

"One of my men is watching the house from across the street a couple of blocks away in a dark-green Ford sedan. He's got a key from the real-estate people, in case it's locked. Talk to him."

"Okay, Chief. And thanks," Frank said.

"One more thing," Collig added. "That garage owner Bilks is an honest and upstanding citizen, as far as we can determine."

"I thought so," Frank replied, then the boys said good-by and hurried to Parker Street. They found the car the chief had described and got the key from the plainclothesman behind the wheel. He assured them again that no one had been near the place.

"Okay," Frank said.

When they entered the house, Joe switched on the lights. "One thing's for sure," he said. "Those footprints weren't made by ghosts!" He pointed to a number of plainly visible heelmarks on the dusty floors. They had a peculiar triangle in the middle.

"The police have been here," Frank reminded him.

"What about these fingermarks on the window sill? They could belong to the man who had taken Chet's dory!"

Certain that the strange symbol on the dory meant that there was a connection between him, John Mead, and the television burglars, Joe wanted to photograph the marks.

It seemed all the more important now, since the case records had been stolen from Mr. Hardy's files.

"I think those prints are worth checking out," Frank agreed. "How about getting our kit?"

Joe drove home and grabbed the equipment. When he returned to 47 Parker Street, the boys set to work.

Taking out a special camera, Joe held it over the sill. He clicked on the lights in it and squinted into the focusing panel. The fingerprints showed up plainly.

"Won't need any powder on these, Frank," he stated.

"Good. I found some marks on this wall but they're not very clear. Think I'll powder them."

While Joe busied himself taking five-, ten-, and fifteen-second time exposures of the marks on the window sill, Frank opened a bottle of gray-colored powder and poured a little on a sheet of paper. Next, he picked up a small camel's-hair brush by the handle and twirled it back and forth between his palms to make it fluffy. Then, after dipping the tip of the brush into the powder, he passed it lightly over the indistinct fingermarks on the wall.

"Ready for the picture, Joe," he announced.

His brother came across the room and made several photographs.

Before putting the camera back into the kit, Joe also took snaps of the various footprints on the floor, then said, "Guess we'd better leave now, Frank, and develop this film."

After a quick but unsuccessful search of the house for other clues or possibly even the secret panel, they left and returned the key to the police officer and went home.

Later, when they had finished printing the pictures in their laboratory, their father walked in.

"Dad!" Joe greeted him, rushing up to his side. "Are you all right?"

"Of course." Mr. Hardy grinned. "Am I not supposed to be?"

His sons looked at him intently. There was a twinkle in his eye.

"You know you are allegedly in a hospital," said Frank. "I'll bet you came home in a disguise."

The detective nodded. "You guessed it."

"Then who was hurt in the warehouse?"

"A dummy. You see, it was evident from the list you found at Bilks' garage, there were two places in this area liable to be hit next. This was one of them. We therefore put a dummy at the night watchman's desk. The guard positioned himself at the rear by the loading gate, and a patrolman watched the place from across the street."

"And still the gang wasn't caught?"

"No. The night watchman was knocked out with gas. The thieves got in before he had a chance to sound the alarm. From the way the dummy looked, they did a good job of knocking him over the head, too."

"And the patrolman?"

"They decoyed him. Set off a fire bomb down the street. When he got out of his car to investigate, one of the gang slipped behind the wheel, pinned the cop to the wall of a factory building, set the brake, and ran off to help the thieves."

"Oh brother!" Joe shook his head.

"By the time a passer-by freed the patrolman, the gang had entered the place, knocked out the guard, and stolen a small truckload of television sets. They worked very efficiently. Couldn't have taken them more than twenty minutes."

"And where were you?" Frank asked.

"Over in Harlington. There's a big appliance outfit which we thought was equally in danger. But nothing happened there."

"And now the thieves think you're out of commission," Frank said.

Mr. Hardy nodded. "This should make them sure enough of themselves so they won't quit now, and hopefully we'll catch them at their next attempt.

"There's one interesting aspect to the whole thing," he added. "The locks were not broken, even though they were quite complicated and so-called burglarproof."

"That means either the thieves had a key, or at least one of them is an expert picklock," Frank deduced.

"Looks that way."

"Another lock was picked recently," Joe put in. "The one to your file cabinet, Dad. The data on the television gang are missing."

Mr. Hardy was very much upset when he heard this, and paced angrily back and forth in front of the window. "There were prints in there which I need and other valuable information!"

"Maybe the marks we photographed a little while ago at Parker Street will help," Frank said.

"No doubt there is a connection between the gang I'm after and the man who sold Chet the dory," Mr. Hardy said. "They might even have used his place as a hideout—or a meeting place."

"Right. But I'm sure this is not where the secret

panel is," Frank said. "And that's where they are holding Lenny Stryker."

"And most likely Martha Johnson," Joe added grimly.

"No answer to that one, yet," Mr. Hardy said. "What's your next move?"

"I think we'll try to track Mike Batton," Frank replied. "After lunch we'll see Ben Whittaker and find out which of his customers were robbed. Batton, no doubt, is connected with the gang, and perhaps some of these people can give us a lead."

"Good thought. Let me know what develops."

The boys left the house a half-hour later and drove to Whittaker's shop. The elderly locksmith was in the rear and greeted them solemnly. He had heard nothing of his former employee.

The police, he told them, had found no trace of the stolen articles. Worse than that, Mrs. Eccles was making matters very unpleasant for him.

"She still threatens legal action if I don't return her money," Whittaker said. "My reputation will be ruined!"

"Oh, no," Frank spoke up quickly. "You've been in business here too many years for something like that to make any difference, Mr. Whittaker."

"But it's not just something!" the man cried out. "There's Mr. Howard, and Mrs. Sommers, and—"

"You mean all those people have been robbed and are making trouble?" Joe asked.

The locksmith nodded. "In each case, Batton went to the house when no one was there but a maid. He used the same story he told you. Oh, what'll I do?"

"Let's go see these people, Frank," Joe said. "Would you give us their addresses, Mr. Whittaker?"

"Sure. The Petersons aren't home, but the others might be able to give you a clue." The man handed them a sheet of paper with the names and addresses on it. "Thanks a lot for your help," he said as they walked out the door.

First they went to see Mr. Howard. He lived alone in a small English Tudor house which he had designed himself.

"That locksmith fellow came when I was out," he told them. "My housekeeper let him in after he claimed I had ordered the lock changed. Well, I hadn't ordered anything of the kind and—"

"We know," Frank interrupted. "We thought you or your housekeeper might remember something Batton said that would give us a clue as to where we can find him."

"Well, let me call Mrs. Curry." Howard left the room and soon returned with an elderly, gray-haired woman. She described Batton, but said she had not spoken to him after she let him in.

"He didn't come into any of the rooms," she explained, "just stayed in the front hall until he changed the lock."

"And that's where the statue was!" Mr. Howard put in. "A rare, hand-carved Oriental piece I paid a lot of money for. He took it, that scoundrel, and I want it back!"

"We understand how you feel," Frank said. "But we'd appreciate it if you could just give us a little time to track down the thief. Chances are your property will be found, once we locate his hideout."

"Well, it all depends how long it will take. Let me know when you find him."

"We certainly will, sir. And thanks for the information."

Next, they called on Mrs. Sommers. The woman appeared upset about the loss of a ring which had been taken from a bureau.

"It was very valuable to me," she told the boys, "for sentimental reasons. A family heirloom. The insurance company will pay for it, but money can never replace it."

Frank asked her about Batton. She could not help them, either. He had changed the lock in her absence. A woman who lived next door had talked to him and told Mrs. Sommers that he had been there.

"Could we speak to your neighbor?" Frank asked.

"She went to visit her son in Missouri two days ago."

Frank and Joe thanked her and left, disappointed. They went to call on Mrs. Eccles, but were equally unsuccessful.

"One thing is clear," Frank told Joe on the way home. "Batton must be in with the television gang, but had his own thing going on the side."

"But why?" Joe asked. "I would think belonging to that outfit would be profitable enough."

"Who knows? Maybe he needed the money now and couldn't wait for the equipment to be sold and the booty divided."

"You suppose he tried to get into our house just to see if there was any dough lying around?"

"No," Frank said thoughtfully. "I have a hunch that he only took the job with Whittaker to get a duplicate key for our place."

"For the gang?"

"Right. You know what we should have done?"

"What?"

"Photographed the fingerprints on Dad's filing cabinet. Ours and his will be there, of course, but there may be strange ones, too!"

"Like Batton's for instance?"

"Could be."

"How are you going to make sure they're his?"

"We'll go back to Mr. Whittaker's shop and check out things Mike Batton has handled, take prints, and compare them!"

"Good thinking!" Joe praised. "Let's do that right away."

The net result of this work was a surprise and added a new complication to the mystery. The man who had rifled Mr. Hardy's files was not Mike Batton!

CHAPTER XIII

The Picklock

"MORE trouble." Frank sighed. "However, we've proved one thing. We probably have the finger-prints of the person who kidnapped Miss John-son."

"Right you are," Joe agreed. "Let's take them over to Chief Collig right away."

Frank quickly wrote a note to his father, telling him about their new discovery, then they delivered the prints to police headquarters.

When they were in their car again, Frank said, "Now for our next job. We'll drive out to the Mead house and see if Chet's dory's there."

"Good idea. But let's stop and get Chet."

They expected to find their stout chum either in the apple orchard or at the Morton refrigerator, but he was at neither place. No one was at home but Mrs. Morton. She seemed surprised to see the Hardys.

"I thought you'd be over at the fair," she remarked.

"What fair?" Frank asked, puzzled.

"Oh, didn't you know about the county fair at Harlington? Chet, Iola and her friends drove over quite a while ago. I understand there are to be all sorts of amusements."

Frank and Joe looked at each other. "We don't really have time—" Frank began.

"Oh, it won't take long to look for Chet," Joe said. "Come on, Frank. Let's go!"

"Okay." The boys hurried to the convertible and sped away. Soon the outlines of a Ferris wheel came in sight.

"Quite a show," Joe remarked as he and Frank got out of the car. Just inside the entrance gate a man standing on a platform was announcing loudly:

"Ten dollars, I said! Ten dollars! Easiest way in the world to earn ten dollars! All you have to be is smart!"

The barker held up a large padlock. "You just have to open this. Sure, it's a trick lock. But it'll cost you only a dime to try. Step this way, gentlemen!"

Frank nudged Joe. The first customer to ascend the stairs was Chet Morton!

The crowd roared with laughter as Chet struggled with the padlock. He seemed determined to win the ten dollars.

"Hey! You better quit before you bust," cried one of the bystanders. Chet was bent double and was very red in the face.

"It'll cost you more than ten dollars for a doctor!" another man shouted.

Frank and Joe were grinning from ear to ear. They knew their friend thought he could open the padlock because he had heard so much about locks and keys lately. But Chet finally gave up and turned away to buy some peanuts.

"Who's next?" called the barker. He pointed his finger directly at the Hardys and added, "You look like a couple of bright fellows. How about coming up here?"

"I sure could use ten dollars," Joe replied, and pushed his way through the crowd.

He struggled with the lock, but to no avail. Disgusted, he handed it back, and Frank ascended the platform.

As Frank, too, failed to open the lock, a tall man about thirty-five years old elbowed his way through the crowd and came up the steps.

Without saying a word he took the lock in his hand, held it near his ear, and shook it. Then he closed his two hands over the lock, worked at it a few seconds, and it opened! The barker stared in blank amazement. Apparently he had not expected anyone to succeed.

"Gimme my money," demanded the stranger.

The barker stared in amazement when the padlock
opened

Reluctantly the carnival man handed over a ten-dollar bill. Frank nudged Joe, and suggested they speak to the picklock.

"Maybe he's on the level, but I don't like his looks," Frank commented.

"Neither do I."

Several people had gathered around the man, but he walked away rapidly and the crowd turned back to watch the next contestant. Frank and Joe ran after him on the pretext of complimenting him on his feat.

"It sure was a swell exhibition." Joe grinned. "I bet that faker never intended to pay out any money."

The tall man did not reply. He kept on walking toward the entrance gate.

"It's my guess you're a locksmith," Frank spoke up. "You must be a good one."

Still the stranger did not speak.

At that moment Chet came running after them. "Hi, fellows!" he yelled.

Frank and Joe were in a panic. They did not want their friend to give away their identity, in case the picklock was connected with the gang they and their father were trying to apprehend.

Frank fell back a step, turned, and put a finger to his lips. Chet caught on at once.

But this precaution did not help for long. As they reached the parking lot outside the exit gates, Iola, Callie, and Helen Osborne ran straight into the group. Smiling affably, Iola called out, "Well, if it isn't Frank and Joe Hardy!"

The man ahead of them muttered something and dodged behind a parked automobile. In a moment he had zigzagged his way out of sight. Frank and Joe dashed after him, but with the confusion of cars coming and going, the wily stranger managed to escape.

"Too bad he got away," Joe said. "But in a way I'm glad this happened. Otherwise we might not really have suspected him. Now I could almost bet he's mixed up with that television gang."

Frank examined the ground nearby. In a minute he was down on his hands and knees, inspecting a heelprint plainly visible in the dust.

"If I'm not mistaken, we're in luck," he said. "Look here! This guy's heelmark is just like the one we photographed at 47 Parker Street."

Joe dropped to his knees, too, and checked out the print. He agreed with his brother.

Just then the girls caught up to them.

"Don't you ever take time out from sleuthing?" Helen teased. She was dark-haired but not as slim as Iola, and shared Chet's interest in food.

"Sure we do," Frank replied, grinning, as he and Joe got to their feet. "But only if there's nothing cooking!"

"Hey," Chet said, rolling his eyes, "that reminds me. What say we meet in the new drugstore downtown for some chow? I'm starved."

"Okay," the Hardys agreed, and started toward their convertible.

"I'll take the girls and meet you in a little while," Chet called, heading for his jalopy.

About fifteen minutes later they walked toward the sandwich counter in the drugstore.

"Chet will treat you all to a full-course dinner," Joe announced with a wink when they sat down.

"Are you kidding?" Chet protested. "I spent most of my money on rides."

"You're safe, Chet." Helen laughed. "We're not hungry, anyway. Had too many hamburgers at the fair."

"I'm thirsty, though," Iola said, a twinkle in her eye.

In the end all the girls decided to have sodas, and the boys ordered sandwiches.

They had almost finished their refreshments when Frank nudged Joe. "That tall man at the counter over there!"

Joe gasped. "The picklock from the fair!"

"*Sh!*" Frank said. "You see what he's buying? Bandage and antiseptic. He might lead us to Lenny Stryker and Martha Johnson!"

"How are we going to work it?"

Frank turned to the others. "Listen," he said tensely. "All of you keep on eating and look down. Don't act surprised at anything you see in the next few minutes. Chet, you'll have to take the girls home."

"Sure, Frank. What are you up to?"

"We've got to trail that guy over there. Joe, after I leave the store, you follow me in the car!"

CHAPTER XIV

Time to Act!

AMAZED, but without question, the Hardys' friends obeyed Frank's instructions.

He quickly crossed the drugstore to a counter of novelties. Without thought to size or color he selected a cap, a pair of sunglasses, and a small mustache. Hastily paying for them, he put on the disguise and dashed for the front door.

Reaching the street, he posted himself just around the corner. A moment later the picklock, carrying his package of bandage and antiseptic, appeared and walked rapidly up the street. Frank followed.

As the man paused by an automobile, Frank wondered if he could possibly get into the back without being noticed. Luck was in his favor, because the man suddenly decided to go to a nearby stand and buy a newspaper. Frank quickly opened the rear door and crouched down on the floor of the car.

The stranger returned, got in, and drove off without seeing him. Frank's heart pounded wildly. He hoped Joe was following him, but he did not dare raise his head to find out.

At the next street intersection the driver pulled up to the curb. A man, who evidently had been waiting for him, jumped into the front seat. When Frank ventured to look up, he caught his breath. The newcomer was none other than the man who had sold Chet the battered dory!

"I thought you'd never make it, Jeff," he said to the driver. "Did you have any trouble?"

"No. But I certainly ain't goin' to be the errand boy no more. Too dangerous. If you want the job, Griff, you can have it."

"Oh, stop moanin'."

"Which way are you goin'?" Griff asked, as the car evidently reached the outskirts of Bayport. He put his arms up on the back of the seat to settle himself more comfortably. Suddenly from the corner of his eye he caught a movement in the back.

"What in the name of—?" he exploded.

Jeff slammed on the brakes, demanding to know what the trouble was. He, too, turned around. By this time Frank had pulled himself up to the back seat. Deciding his only chance now was to put on an act, he grinned stupidly at the two men.

"Don't mind me," he said in a high shrill voice.

"I love to ride. And wadda you think? Nobody ever asks me!"

The two men looked at each other, then back at the "moron" in their car.

"Aw, go on," the boy pleaded. "And go real fast, too. I like to go fast!"

Jeff's eyes closed until they were mere slits. His jaws snapped shut. "Get out!" he hissed.

"Why, what've I done?" Frank whined. "You wouldn't put me out when I've only been ridin' five minutes."

The man named Griff was inclined to be lenient, but Jeff would not have it. "Out!" he said, and leaning back, opened one of the rear doors. Griff, taking the cue, gave Frank a shove and he landed at the side of the road. Then the car roared away.

Frank leaped to his feet. Seconds later Joe came along in the convertible. Frank jumped in beside his brother and they raced after the fleeing automobile.

At a crossroads the boys lost time trying to decide which way the suspects had gone. Tire tracks indicated they might have taken the road which led directly to the bay, so Joe followed it to the end.

"I'm afraid they got away," he said in disappointment as they neared the water. Just ahead was the public dock of the Bayport Steamship

Company, and some distance from shore was an outgoing ferry.

"You mean the car went on that ferry?" Frank asked.

"Yes."

While Frank removed his disguise, Joe inquired at the office about the ferry's destination. The boys' worst fears were confirmed. They could not possibly circle the bay to the ferry's next stop before the boat would dock and the suspects' car vanish.

In disgust the boys returned home and tumbled into bed early. A sound night's sleep refreshed them, and in the morning they were ready for action again. As they were dressing, Frank suddenly snapped his fingers.

"Say, Joe," he said, "maybe those men never went on that ferry after all. What say we go back there and look around?"

"Smartest idea you've had in a week!" Joe dodged the pillow Frank hurled at him.

The boys hurried downstairs. They were disappointed to learn that their father had remained out of town overnight, and had left word that he would not return home until midmorning.

Frank and Joe had hardly seated themselves at the breakfast table when Chet came through the doorway from the kitchen, glaring at them irately.

"Chet! Aren't you up kind of early?" Joe gibed.
The boy ignored the question. "I'm here to

collect four dollars and thirty cents," he announced, without smiling.

"Wow!" cried Joe. "It sounds like a damage suit."

"Well, you might call it that," Chet said. "Anyway, you fellows have to fork over the money."

"And why?"

"You forgot to pay for your meal last night. On top of that you invited the girls to have sodas, and" —Chet pointed his finger accusingly—"and you left me the check!"

Frank and Joe burst into laughter. "So that's it?" said Joe. "Why, you ungrateful wretch! We left you with three of Bayport's most beautiful girls. What's four dollars and thirty cents compared to that?"

"It was a fine idea," said Chet, "only I didn't have enough money with me. Had to borrow from my sister. And did she kid me! Well, hand over the cash!"

"How about a compromise?" Frank asked, winking at Joe. "We'll pay two-thirds. In return for the rest you can have breakfast here and then go with us to nab that boat thief you're after. His name's Griff."

Chet's eyes opened wide. He forgot his troubles at once, and demanded to be brought up to date on news of his case. Upon hearing the account of Frank's adventure the evening before, Chet was eager to start off at once on the trail of the thief.

Even Aunt Gertrude was amused at his refusal of a second helping of fried apple rings and corn bread.

By nine o'clock the three friends were on their way in the convertible. Frank made no stops until they came to a red traffic light some distance out of town. The signal began to hum peculiarly as it changed to green.

"Another singing light!" Joe exclaimed. "Maybe ten minutes' drive from here—"

"Now listen, fellows," Chet interrupted, "you promised we'd hunt for that man Griff—"

"Okay," Frank said, and turned right.

Two minutes later they reached the public dock where the Hardys had lost the men the evening before. The boys jumped out and began to search in the roadway for clues.

Joe was the first to notice a narrow dirt road which branched off to the left along the water's edge. Judging from tall patches of grass growing in it, the road was not used often. But there was a set of freshly made tire tracks.

"Come over here!" Joe called excitedly, and pointed out his discovery. "These may mean something. Let's follow them!"

The three hopped into the car. Almost unconsciously Joe glanced at his watch, for he had become accustomed to timing their ten-minute rides from the "singing" traffic lights. Now he subtracted two minutes. Where would they be in eight more?

The road twisted and turned, finally coming out on the highway. Here the tire marks Frank had been following became intermingled with others.

Joe was excited. "Go on, Frank!" he cried. Two minutes later Joe called a halt and pointed.

"At last," he yelled, "we've solved it!"

"Solved what?" Chet demanded.

Words tumbled from Joe's lips. Just ahead was the Mead mansion, and they were ten minutes' drive from singing light number three!

"Remember when we were checking the fuse box and you got a shock that knocked you cold?" Joe asked Frank.

"Sure do."

"When I was in the library I heard a groan and raced back to you in the kitchen, thinking something had happened to you."

Frank looked startled. "I didn't groan. It was someone else!"

"Exactly!"

"Say, would you fellows mind telling me what you're talking about?" Chet demanded.

"Sure we'll tell you," Joe replied. "There's probably a hidden room in the Mead house. You get into it through a secret panel. And behind that panel are the two people who have been kidnapped."

"I'll bet you're right!" Frank agreed, his heart pounding. "Lenny Stryker and Martha Johnson! I'd better hide the car in case anyone's watching. We'll go the rest of the way on foot."

"Now listen, fellows," Chet spoke up, "you're not going to get me mixed up in anything dangerous. I only came along to find that guy who got my money and then stole my boat."

"Chet has a point there," said Frank. "Suppose we go by a roundabout route to the Mead boathouse first and see if the dory's there?"

Chet trailed the Hardys through a patch of woods to the water's edge. Then, creeping forward on their hands and knees, the boys made their way cautiously along the bank to the boathouse. Certain that no one had seen them, Frank stripped off his clothes and swam under the door of the building. Minutes later he returned, his eyes shining excitedly.

"It's in there!" he whispered hoarsely. "The dory with the funny Y on it!"

"Gosh! You mean it?" Chet whooped.

"Quiet!" Joe hissed. "Do you want to spoil everything?"

"Time to act!" Frank said tersely. "Chet, you take the car and bring Dad here at once. Tell him to give our special Hardy rap on the front door. Joe, you and I'll go inside the house and look for the secret panel!"

CHAPTER XV

Prisoners

CHET left at once, returning to the main road by the route through the woods. He sighed in relief as he reached the convertible and opened the door. Another twenty minutes and—

"Hold it!" A voice hissed in his ear and a hand was laid on his shoulder.

Chet's heart almost stopped beating as he was pulled around roughly and stood looking into a leering face.

Griff!

"Finally we've got you snoopers where we want you!" the man growled. "Come along. You're goin' to spend a little time with me while the boss takes care of those friends of yours, the Hardys!"

Frank and Joe, meanwhile, stealthily made their way to the Mead mansion. Using the boathouse as a cover, then the shrubbery, they finally reached the mansion without walking in the open.

While Frank unlocked the front door, Joe kept a sharp lookout. They were sure nobody had seen them.

Noiselessly the door swung open. They stepped into the somber hall. This time, as a precaution against alerting anyone to their presence, they did not try the lights. Knowing their way around, they quickly tiptoed from room to room. Satisfied that no one was in the house, they began to hunt for a secret panel.

Not a word was spoken. Taking it for granted that the secret opening was somewhere near where Joe had heard the groan, the boys concentrated their efforts on the library. Dividing the work, they started to examine the walls inch by inch.

Every bit of dark, ornate molding was scrutinized. They ran their fingertips lightly over the paneling that gave off the smothery smell of dust. Frank stifled a sneeze in his handkerchief.

Several minutes ticked by, then Joe quietly left the library and went to the front door. He opened it slightly and looked out. Squinting, he studied every bush. All was still.

He returned to Frank and whispered, "The coast is still clear. Nothing is stirring outside."

"Okay. We've covered everything but the fireplace and the walls on either side of it!" Frank got up from his knees and stretched his aching back. The floor molding had yielded nothing. He looked at his watch and was startled to find that they had been in the house for an hour.

"I wonder where Dad is," he whispered.

Joe shrugged. "We're not finished yet, anyway."

"He must have been out when Chet got there. I hope he comes soon."

Once more the boys went to work. It was almost an hour later when Frank—tapping, pushing, and pulling at bits of the heavily carved paneling near the fireplace—made a discovery. On a design of an oak tree, one leaf proved to be movable. Beneath it was a metal disk.

"Hey, Joe, I've found something!" he said in a hushed tone.

Joe leaped across the room to his brother. "What in the world is that?" he asked, surprised.

"I don't know. It's not a keyhole, that's for sure."

Together the boys tried to slide the disk aside, but were unsuccessful. Suddenly Frank had an inspiration. Pulling his compass from his pocket, he held it near the disk. There was a definite attraction between the piece of metal and the compass needle!

"A big magnet must make this thing work!" Frank concluded. "Maybe there's one hidden somewhere in this room."

Joe grinned. "What a wild guess! Besides, we've

checked this room so thoroughly that we certainly would have found it!"

Nonetheless Frank began to search, moving slowly about the room. Suddenly the compass slipped from his hands and landed on the rug with a dull thud.

Frank bent over to pick it up, but drew his hand back when the compass moved. "Holy crow! Am I dreaming? This thing has legs!"

"What do you mean?" Joe stared at the compass. It slid over the floor as if by magic. "This place must be hexed!"

"Maybe not," Frank replied. "The compass could be pulled by the magnet I dreamed up."

"You're a genius, Frank!"

Both boys fell to their knees and examined the floor. Joe, too, was convinced now that a large magnet must be hidden underneath. They pulled up a corner of the rug where the compass had stopped moving. After a frantic search they found a board which was not nailed in place. Lifting it, they grinned in delight. On a beam lay a large magnet!

"I'll try it against the wall!" Frank said, picking up the heavy piece of steel. He hurried to the metal disk and directed the magnet toward it. Suddenly there was a clicking sound. At the same moment a large section of the wall on which the tree was carved began to slide.

The secret panel!

Frank and Joe held their breath. As the opening became larger they found themselves peering into a room. They gulped in amazement. On a cot lay a young man. Beside him stood the missing nurse, Martha Johnson!

Joe was first to step over the threshold of the secret room. As the woman recognized him, terror came into her eyes.

"No! No!" she cried out. "Don't come in!"

The warning was spoken too late. Two men had been lying in wait for them on either side of the panel, poised to attack.

Frank and Joe, taken unaware, fought like tigers, but a third member of the gang appeared from the library and joined in the fracas. Frank and Joe were overpowered. They recognized two of the men. *Griff and Jeff!*

"We've got you at last!" Jeff panted. "That's the end of your meddling in our affairs!"

In the meantime Miss Johnson had edged toward the doorway, hoping to escape. But Griff caught her arm.

"Oh, no, you don't!" he hissed. "You're not going anywhere!"

The boys were bound hand and foot, and left on the floor. The criminals surveyed their work, satisfied grins on their faces.

An agonized groan came from the patient on the cot. Griff began to laugh hoarsely.

"You can have that sick kid all to yourselves now," he jeered. "You been wantin' to find him!"

He picked up the magnet from the floor. "Come on, men," he said, then turned to the others. "You won't be able to get out of here—unless I let you. And I don't intend to!"

The three men stepped through the opening into the library. As the Hardys watched in horror, the secret panel closed.

They were prisoners!

CHAPTER XVI

Double Trouble

A<small>FTER</small> Griff and Jeff and their accomplice had left, Miss Johnson deftly began to unfasten the ropes which bound the Hardys. As soon as they were free, the boys dashed to the panel and tried to open it.

"It's no use," the woman told them. "I've tried and tried."

"And there's no other way out of this room?" Frank asked.

The nurse said there was not a window or door in the place. She had searched in vain.

"But fresh air gets in here somehow," Frank pointed out.

"I've concluded it comes through the ceiling. But, as you see, that's very high and there's no way to get up to it."

Frank and Joe were annoyed with themselves

for being trapped. Their only hope now was that Chet had reached their father and that he would be able to figure out how to open the panel.

"But maybe Jeff and Griff will take the magnet with them," Joe said apprehensively.

The boys looked and looked for a means of escape, but could find none. Finally they sat down on the floor to talk over the situation.

"Please tell us everything that happened to you after you left our house," Joe said to the nurse.

Before Martha Johnson could begin her story, the youth on the cot groaned again, and tried to get up. The nurse rushed to his side and held him down. She asked Frank to get a tablet and a glass of water from the table and give it to the patient. In a few moments he became quiet.

"Lenny Stryker, no doubt," Frank said.

"Yes. How did you know?" Miss Johnson asked.

"Conjecture. We've been looking for him."

"This boy is dreadfully ill," Miss Johnson went on. "He should be in a hospital."

"Can we ask him some questions?"

"It wouldn't do any good. He has such a high temperature that he's delirious most of the time."

"How did you find out who he is, then?" asked Joe.

"I heard the name mentioned. I don't know how he got mixed up with those awful people. They were afraid to let him go because he might have notified the police."

"Do the three men come here often?" Frank asked.

The nurse stated that at least one of them came once every day to bring food and anything needed for Lenny. No one had ever stayed very long until the night before. Then the tall one called Jeff had posted himself in the room.

"I was sure something was going to happen," she said. "That's why I had an eye on the secret panel when it began to open. Oh, I wish you hadn't gotten yourselves into this trouble!"

Frank and Joe tried to reassure her. They mentioned having sent Chet Morton to bring Mr. Hardy.

"Suppose your friend never reached him?"

"Why do you say that?" Joe asked.

Miss Johnson said that she had overheard the men talking about posting guards on the grounds. The boys' spirit sank.

"Maybe Chet is a prisoner himself somewhere now," Frank said worriedly.

"That would account for Dad's not getting here," Joe added. Then a worse thought struck him. "Suppose Dad's a prisoner, too!"

Martha Johnson looked desperate. "What are we going to do?"

"Right now all we can do is sit tight and wait," Frank said.

Joe changed the subject. "How did they get you here, Miss Johnson?"

The nurse told how she had been captured right after leaving the Hardy home. Someone on the street had started to pass her, then whirled around and grabbed her arm. She had screamed, and a chloroform-drenched handkerchief had been held against her face. When she regained consciousness, she was in an automobile, and a short while later was imprisoned in the hidden room.

"I still have no idea where I am," she said.

Frank and Joe told her. Miss Johnson had never heard of the mansion, and was intrigued to learn that the owner had installed doors and windows without visible hardware.

They discussed the strange history of the Mead house for a while, but as time went by, their fears increased. So did their hunger. They wondered if anyone would bring food. There seemed little likelihood of this now, because the thieves no doubt would make their escape while they had a chance.

"Did anyone come besides the three men we saw today?" Frank asked the nurse.

"Yes. One they called the Boss. He's about fifty, tall, and slender."

"Did you hear them say anything that might shed some more light on their operation?" Joe asked.

"They talked very little," Miss Johnson answered. "But I remember that they said they would make their getaway as soon as possible and give up this whole area."

The Hardys were glumly silent as they realized the thieves probably were on their way by this time.

Lenny Stryker was stirring again. Suddenly he leaped from his cot. Wild-eyed, he began to limp around the room, mumbling to himself.

Miss Johnson and the boys caught hold of him and put him back on the cot.

A moment later the light went out. Lenny became quiet at once, and for several seconds there was absolute silence. Then came an indistinct grating noise. The panel was being opened!

Quickly the boys made their way toward the spot. Frank whipped out his flashlight. But before he could snap it on, Lenny got up again and knocked it to the floor. Screaming and waving his arms, the delirious young man kept the others from reaching the entranceway.

During the confusion the Hardys heard a thud, then a slight click. The light went on again. They gasped as they saw Chet sprawled on the floor!

He looked up in terror, then recognized them.

"Oh, it's you! Am I glad!"

Chet's momentary elation faded when the Hardys did not return his enthusiasm. They pointed to the closed panel, to Lenny Stryker who now lay in a heap on the floor, and introduced Miss Johnson.

"Gosh!" Chet cried. "Let's get out of here!"

"We can't," Frank told him. "Did you contact Dad?"

Chet shook his head, his eyes roving around the room. Then he caught on. Joe nodded, confirming that they were locked in.

"We're behind the secret panel which can't be opened except with a large magnet. And that magnet isn't here."

The stout boy gulped and sat down on the floor. Looking up at his friends, he asked, "What are we going to do?"

"Suppose you tell us what happened to you," Frank said.

After they lifted Lenny to the cot, Chet related how he had got no farther than the Hardys' car before being captured. He had been taken to the Mead boathouse and locked inside.

"I've been there ever since," he said. "At least that guy Griff brought me some food. Oh—"

Chet stopped speaking as he suddenly remembered something. From his jacket pockets he pulled out several candy bars, an apple, and a small box of crackers. "I never go anywhere without my emergency rations," he said, smiling. He passed them around. For once Chet did not talk about being hungry himself, and insisted the others eat every bit of the food.

"Isn't there any way at all to get out of this room?" he asked desperately.

"None that we've discovered so far," Frank told him. "But let's try again."

While the nurse attended to the patient who was mumbling again, the Hardys made another minute examination of the paneled woodwork in the room. But every piece of carved design seemed to be solidly placed.

They had almost decided to give up the search when Frank came to a section on the right side of the panel where a bird had been cut into the wood. It was perched on a tree branch about five and a half feet above the floor. Frank studied its head and body carefully. Then he put his finger on its heavily feathered wing and gently pushed it up. The wing moved!

CHAPTER XVII

The Wreck

"COME here!" Frank cried excitedly.

The others leaped to his side. Miss Johnson turned the lamp so that its light shone directly on the bird. Beneath its wing, three tiny slits were revealed.

"The symbol!" Joe exclaimed. "The strange Y!"

For several moments everyone stared in amazement.

"What is it?" Martha Johnson asked.

Frank looked toward Lenny Stryker and put his fingers to his lips. The nurse assured him that her patient was now asleep and could not overhear anything.

"I don't know what the strange mark means," Frank explained. "But we've seen it several times and think it's a clue to a gang of thieves. Somehow Lenny Stryker got mixed up with them."

"And you think this house is their headquarters?" Miss Johnson asked.

"It looks that way," Joe replied.

Frank told her how they met the Englishman who claimed to be John Mead and about the key he had evidently lost when his car landed in a ditch.

"He wore a ring with this symbol," Frank said. "Did you happen to notice whether any of the men who came here wore such a ring?"

After a moment's thought Miss Johnson said she could not be sure. The tall man called the Boss had worn a large signet ring, but she had not noticed the design. She recalled, however, that he had mentioned the name Carr Electronics once.

"Carr Electronics?" Frank repeated. "That's where the dummy was hit over the head when the place was burglarized."

"What about the symbol under the bird's wing?" Joe asked. "I'm sure it's not just here for decorative purposes."

"There might be something hidden beyond it," Frank agreed. "But what?" He worked on the slits for a while, but finally gave up. Joe and Chet each took a turn. Even Miss Johnson, intrigued by the idea, tried her hand at it.

Hours dragged by. The prisoners became hungry and discouraged. They took turns pounding on the secret panel but doubted that their signals would be heard by anyone.

"It's eleven P.M.," groaned Chet. "We've been gone from your house fourteen hours!"

Back home, meanwhile, Mrs. Hardy and Aunt Gertrude were frantic with worry. They had not thought much about the boys' absence until evening. Mr. Hardy had gone out again and could not be reached. Unable to stand the strain any longer, Mrs. Hardy finally went to the telephone and called Mrs. Morton.

"Hello," she said, trying to seem calm. After a few pleasantries she asked, "Is Chet there?"

"No, he's not, Laura. Isn't he with Frank and Joe?"

Mrs. Hardy revealed with a sinking heart that Chet had left the house with her sons directly after breakfast and she had not heard from any of them since.

"It's unusual for them not to telephone if they're going to stay out late," Mrs. Hardy said. "But I'm sure they'll be home soon," she added, in order not to alarm Mrs. Morton more than was necessary.

"Oh, I hope so," Chet's mother replied anxiously. "Those boys sometimes get into such dangerous situations. Please let me know the minute you hear from them."

"I'll phone you if I get any news," Mrs. Hardy assured her friend.

She had barely said good-by when the telephone rang. It was Chief Collig.

"Mrs. Hardy," he asked brusquely, "are Frank and Joe there?"

"No, Chief. Is anything wrong?"

"Then let me speak to Fenton," Collig went on, pretending that he had not heard her anxious question.

"He's not here, either. Oh, wait a minute," she added, hearing a key in the lock. "Fenton's just coming in the door."

Mrs. Hardy called her husband to the telephone.

"Thank you, dear. Who is it?" he asked.

"Chief Collig."

Mr. Hardy's eyebrows lifted as he took the phone. "Yes, Chief?" As he listened to Collig, his few grew grave.

"Have you tried the hospitals? . . . They're not there? . . . I'll be right over."

The news was disturbing. The officer had reported that the boys' overturned convertible had been found in a ditch some miles out of Bayport. There had been no sign of either Frank or Joe, and no report of the accident.

Laura Hardy's hand flew to her mouth to stifle a cry. Aunt Gertrude began spluttering about her dire predictions coming true. "This detective work is too risky for boys." As she took off her glasses to wipe them, her hands shook.

"When did you last hear from the boys?" Mr. Hardy asked his wife. Upon being told, his face clouded. "Well, I'm going to police headquarters."

"You know something you're not telling me," his wife cried, grabbing his arm as he was about to go out the door.

"I have a hunch the car was stolen," he replied. "I want to drive to the spot where it was abandoned and see if I can pick up any clues."

Aunt Gertrude wailed, "Hurry! Hurry! They've probably been kidnapped!"

The detective was out of the house before Mrs. Hardy could voice any further questions, and rushed to headquarters.

Collig was not scheduled to be on duty, but when the report of the overturned Hardy car had come in, the chief had rushed to his office.

When Mr. Hardy arrived, he jumped up from his leather chair, his forehead creased with frown lines. "This really has me worried, Fenton."

"Come on. Hop in my car," the detective said.

They sped to the scene of the accident, about five miles west of Bayport. With flashlights, the two men carefully examined the rough ground for any sign of a clue. There were no footprints.

"That's strange," Collig grunted. "We haven't had any rain to wash 'em away, either!"

Mr. Hardy did not speak. Slowly he walked

back along the road in the direction from which the car had come. Reaching a spot about one hundred feet from the convertible, he played his flashlight over the area and found a set of footprints.

"Here's your answer," he called out. "Pretty daring person."

It was the detective's belief that the driver of the car had jumped and let it go on to wreck itself. Obviously he was neither one of his sons nor Chet Morton.

"It's a real relief to know that," Mr. Hardy concluded, "but it doesn't find the boys. I'm going back to town now and start a search."

Collig had his own plan of operation, so the men separated after their return to police headquarters. Mr. Hardy drove at once to 47 Parker Street and examined the house carefully. When it yielded no results, he continued on to various spots which he had had under surveillance in connection with the television thieves. But the outcome of his investigation was discouraging.

Tired and worried, he finally went home at eight in the morning. Refreshing himself with a hasty breakfast and some coffee, he asked his wife to pack some sandwiches, then started out again. Mrs. Hardy and Aunt Gertrude, who had slept only fitfully, asked what he intended to do next.

"I'm driving to the Mead house," he replied,

*Mr. Hardy and Chief Collig examined the ground
for clues*

masking his concern. "I've an idea the boys found out something over there and are still sleuthing around the place."

He did not tell the two women his real fears. By now he was convinced that his sons and Chet were in the hands of the very men he was trying to capture!

CHAPTER XVIII

Holding a Suspect

WITHIN an hour after Mr. Hardy had left home on his search for Frank and Joe, the doorbell rang. Hoping the caller would have good news, Aunt Gertrude dashed to answer it. A lean man in his thirties stood outside.

"Is this the Hardy house?" he asked, smiling, and took off his hat. Learning that it was, he added, "Are Frank and Joe at home?"

"No," Aunt Gertrude replied.

"When do you expect them?"

"Suppose you tell me your name and why you wish to see them."

"I'm John Mead."

Aunt Gertrude reeled. She put one hand to her forehead and grasped the door with the other.

"You seem surprised to hear that," the stranger remarked. "Is there something peculiar about it?"

"I—I—We thought you were dead!"

The caller laughed. "Me dead? I'm very much alive. What gave you that idea?"

By this time Gertrude Hardy had steadied her nerves. She had heard enough about the mystery her brother and the boys were trying to solve to know that the person who stood before her might be one of the suspects in the case. She was hesitant about inviting him into the house; yet she was fearful of letting him go.

As calmly as possible she finally asked him to come inside. Calling loudly for her sister-in-law, she escorted John Mead into the living room. The boys' mother hurried in.

"Laura, this is Mr. John Mead," Aunt Gertrude announced.

Mrs. Hardy felt faint, but she tried not to show it. The three sat down. It immediately became evident to the caller that the two women were very nervous.

"My coming here seems to have upset you," he said. "Last Monday I met Frank and Joe Hardy on the road. I had trouble with my car and they kindly helped me out."

The women nodded.

"I just returned and am on the way home. So I stopped by to thank them again and invite them over to the house. It's an interesting old place and I thought they'd get a kick out of it."

He stopped speaking, expecting one or the

other to say something, but both Mrs. Hardy and
Aunt Gertrude remained silent. They were staring at a ring he wore on his right hand. This was
the first time they had seen the strange Y symbol.
Suddenly Mrs. Hardy realized that the awkward
pause had been rather long.

"Oh—ah—yes," she said. "The boys told us
about you. But they're not at home now and I
don't know when they'll be back."

Aunt Gertrude again brought up the subject of
how they had heard that John Mead, who owned
the house on the bay, had died five years ago in a
car accident.

"I see what you mean." The caller smiled. "He
was my uncle."

"Your uncle!" Mrs. Hardy cried. "We thought
he had no relatives."

"I suppose everyone thought that," John Mead
went on. "To tell you the truth, my uncle was a
rather eccentric man and people knew little about
him. He was not married, and my father and I
were his only relatives. We lived in England most
of our lives.

"About five years ago I received a strange note
from Uncle John. He wrote that he was sending
me a box and would explain its contents later. He
wanted to be sure of my receiving the gifts before
telling me what they were."

The visitor explained that the box had contained the ring he wore and some odd-looking

keys. That was all. He had written to his uncle at the Bayport address saying the package had come, but he had never gotten a reply.

"Apparently Uncle John died before receiving my letter. But I didn't know this until much later. It seems no will was found, but my father had once told me my wealthy relative was leaving everything to me. Recently I arrived in this country and came here to Bayport last week to see my uncle's estate."

Though the stranger seemed honest, the two women were still suspicious. While Mrs. Hardy continued the conversation, Aunt Gertrude quietly left the room and went upstairs to telephone police headquarters.

Chief Collig, still out on a personal search for Frank and Joe, was not available, but the sergeant on duty promised to send a plainclothesman at once.

During Miss Hardy's absence from the living room, the boys' mother inquired about the condition of the Mead mansion. She remembered her sons talking about the fact that the electricity had been turned on and off at various times.

"Since the house has been abandoned for so long, I'm sure all the utilities are shut off," she said, looking at the caller intently. "How did you live there when you arrived?"

"I didn't stay very long," Mead replied, "and I

didn't bother turning it on. Just used a flashlight on my brief tour through the house. I do hope the generator is still in working order. My father told me about it."

He then went on to describe the intricate locks his uncle had devised, and his own discovery of the various secret mechanisms.

"That's one of the things I thought your boys would enjoy looking at," he concluded.

A few minutes later the doorbell rang. Aunt Gertrude hurried to admit the plainclothesman. Quickly she whispered her suspicions to him, then brought him into the living room. She introduced the police officer as a friend, preventing Mrs. Hardy from asking questions by a conspiratorial glance.

"Well, I'd better be going," John Mead said. "Please tell Frank and Joe I'd like to see them soon."

As he started to leave, the plainclothesman blocked his way. "I'd like to ask you a few questions," he said.

For several minutes the detective quizzed the Englishman, but learned nothing from him other than what he had told the two women. Finally John Mead became irritated.

"You'd think I was some sort of criminal!" he burst out. "I know this is a detective's home, and you probably think everybody who comes here is a suspect of some kind, but I can't see why I warrant such treatment!"

"Well, if you must know, you *are* a suspect!" Aunt Gertrude exclaimed.

"What?" John Mead looked as if someone had struck him. He recovered in a moment, however, and demanded to know what she meant. Mrs. Hardy tried to calm her unexpected visitor.

"Please sit down again, Mr. Mead," she said. "We'll tell you the story."

"This man is a detective," Aunt Gertrude explained. "If you try any funny business—"

"I don't know what you're talking about," Mead replied. "Funny business indeed, but on your side! I insist upon knowing why you are virtually holding me a prisoner!" His eyes blazed angrily.

"That ring you are wearing bears the insignia of a gang of thieves!" Miss Hardy cried excitedly. "How do we know you're not one of them?"

John Mead turned pale. Nervously he insisted he was not a thief, and that he had received the ring by mail from his uncle years ago.

"Your story could be true and it could not," the plainclothesman spoke up. "But if you're going to the Mead house I'm coming with you."

"And we are too!" chorused the women.

They thought it best not to mention the fact that Mr. Hardy was out there searching for the boys. Moreover, they were so worried about Frank and Joe they wanted to find out if there was any news.

Mead looked from one to the other, then shrugged. "Come along, then. I have nothing to hide!"

The plainclothesman drove the four in a police car. When they reached the Mead house, they found Mr. Hardy and two policemen still trying to find a way to get into the mansion. The detective was surprised to see his wife and sister, and even more so to meet John Mead. He questioned him closely and decided his story was plausible.

Mead, meanwhile, had realized the seriousness of the situation and was very cooperative.

"We have reason to believe there's trouble inside the house, and that my sons are being held prisoners here," Mr. Hardy explained. "I was just about to break in. Do you have a key?"

"Yes. I lost one, but I have three more for the other doors."

The detective led the way to the back door of the mansion and Mead opened it.

"It took me quite a while to find out how to get in," the Englishman explained.

Mr. Hardy nodded. "It's a strange setup." Inside, he clicked a wall switch and the lights went on.

"That's odd," said Mead. "I thought—"

"Someone else knows about the generator," Mr. Hardy explained. Then he turned to the others.

"The two officers and I will make a thorough search of the house. You'd better wait here."

The three went off and returned after a while, reporting that they had not found a trace of the boys.

"You may as well go home," Mr. Hardy told his wife and sister. "Thomas here," he added, referring to the plainclothesman, "can take you back. I'd like Mr. Mead to stay. We'll look around again."

After the women had left he gave Mead a sketchy account of the mystery on which he was working. He revealed the part Lenny Stryker had played in it, the kidnapping of Martha Johnson, and how the only clue to the boys' whereabouts lay in the secret panel.

"All trails lead to this house," he concluded. "Think carefully, Mr. Mead. Did your uncle ever mention a secret panel to you?"

Mead shook his head, dumbfounded. He had no idea the mansion contained anything of a secret nature other than the hidden locks on the doors and windows, but he could well imagine that his eccentric relative might have built a hidden room.

"Uncle John was very withdrawn, my father told me. Perhaps he had a secret room where he worked. But I never heard of one."

Mr. Hardy was inclined to believe that the Englishman was telling the truth. Nevertheless, he signaled to one of the policemen, whose name was Mac, to keep close watch on him and see that he did not escape.

Then the detective went outside with the other officer and surveyed the house carefully. They decided that architecturally the most likely place to build a secret room would be off the library.

Before they went back inside, they moved the cars so they would be concealed. Then they began a careful examination of the carved paneling in the library.

Mr. Hardy called his sons' names a few times, but there was no response.

"If they were somewhere near here, wouldn't they hear us?" Mac asked.

"Not necessarily. They could be gagged. Or the panel could be soundproof. Joe heard a groan once, but at that time he was not in this room, and the panel could have been open."

Mr. Hardy focused his attention on the fireplace and the walls on either side of it. His eyes wandered, and it was not long before he located the oak tree with its movable leaf.

Before he could investigate the metal disk beneath, Mac, who stood near the hall door, detected a slight sound. Instantly he signaled the others to put them on guard. Turning off the light, Mr. Hardy and the two policemen ducked behind the heavy draperies, pulling Mead with them.

The front door opened and closed again. Footsteps sounded along the hallway. Finally a man came stealthily into the library and walked toward the fireplace. The four watched intently in the dimness.

Was the intruder going to open the secret panel?

CHAPTER XIX

Closing In

THE man who had entered the Mead home carried a large package under his arm. He hid it inside the fireplace and turned away.

The detectives and John Mead watched him tensely. To their disappointment he did not touch the paneled wall; instead, he walked back toward the hall.

At that instant Mr. Hardy leaped from hiding and pinned the man's arms behind him. Startled, the stranger tried to wrench himself free, but was confronted by the policemen. One of them turned on the light.

Mr. Hardy stared closely at the prisoner. From the description Frank and Joe had given him, the man could be Mike Batton, the dishonest locksmith.

"Okay, Batton, calm down," Mr. Hardy said.

"How do you—?" the fellow began, then

stopped short and turned to the policemen. "Take your hands off me!" he cried.

"What are you doing here?" John Mead demanded.

"I could ask you the same question," Batton replied with a sneer.

"Open that package!" Mr. Hardy ordered him. At first Mike only stared back insolently and did not obey. When he was told the police were looking for him and it would go still harder with him if he did not cooperate, he changed his mind.

He pulled the string from the bundle by the fireplace. Several bracelets, rings, and necklaces rolled out.

"Where did you get this jewelry?" Mr. Hardy asked.

"I'm not telling."

Under further questioning, though, Batton admitted that he had stolen it because he needed money to pay a large gambling debt.

"I know a guy who buys stolen gems," he said. "Soon as he shows up, he'll pay me a lot of money for them."

"He's coming here? When?" Mr. Hardy inquired.

Batton suddenly looked frightened and did not answer.

"Put him under arrest," Mr. Hardy said to the police, and advised the prisoner of his rights.

"Now give me the key you used to get in here!" he demanded of him.

Batton refused. The two officers searched him. In his pockets they found a key ring with several keys on it, also a single, new-looking one. He admitted that it fitted the back door.

"Where did you get it?" Mr. Hardy asked.

"A friend gave it to me," Batton replied. "He said the house belonged to him, but he wasn't using it, and I could stay here whenever I wanted to."

"Is that the same friend who will buy your loot?"

"Ah—yes, yes, he is."

"What's his name?"

"Jack."

"Jack what?"

"Don't know. He never told me his last name."

"Where does he live?"

"Don't know."

Batton would reveal no more and Mr. Hardy asked Mac to take him into the kitchen for the time being and handcuff him to the door handle of the refrigerator.

"I don't believe a word he said about his friend," the detective muttered. Then he renewed his investigation of the disk behind the oak leaf in the paneling.

Almost immediately he was startled by the attraction of his stainless-steel watch to the metal piece on the wall. He searched the room for a powerful magnet, lifted the rug, and presently found the loose floor board.

It was only a matter of seconds before the secret panel moved. Mr. Hardy gazed into the room beyond and breathed a sigh of relief.

"Dad!" Frank and Joe cried in unison.

"Hi, boys!" Mr. Hardy was thankful to see his sons and Chet unharmed. Quickly he explained about John Mead and greeted Miss Johnson, who was elated about the rescue.

"I thought we'd be here forever," she said with a grateful smile.

Frank introduced the patient on the cot. "Dad, this is Lenny Stryker."

The young man, whose fever had diminished greatly in the early-morning hours, sat up. "I feel terrible about the whole thing," he said weakly.

"Don't try to talk," Frank told him. "I'll explain."

Lenny had revealed his experiences to the boys a little while before, and Frank related them to his father. The boy's uncle had asked him if he would like a job to earn some money on the side to help his mother. The offer had been a trick.

After being introduced by his uncle to several men, Lenny realized they were about to rob an appliance warehouse. He wanted no part in it but was forced to go along.

He was so nervous that he could not carry out his assignment to take away the guard's gun. He had started to run and the watchman had shot him in the leg.

"I can't understand," Chet put in, "why your uncle should want an inexperienced person along on such a big job."

"I guess he was trying to get even with my mother," Lenny told him. "He's my father's half brother and wanted to marry her. But she didn't like him and now I can see why. I guess she knows he isn't on the level."

Mr. Hardy nodded. "That explains a great deal. Is your uncle Whitey Masco—or rather Judd Merk?"

"You know!" Lenny cried out in alarm.

"Masco was an alias?" Frank asked in surprise.

"Yes. Unfortunately I didn't find out until yesterday, or we might have cracked this case sooner."

"Do I have to go to jail now?" Lenny asked in a frightened voice.

"I don't think so," Mr. Hardy replied. "First you'll be taken to the hospital. You'll be in police custody, but I'm sure everything will turn out all right. Don't worry, Lenny."

As for his uncle's activities, Lenny could offer little. He had no knowledge of Merk's personal life, and most of the boy's harrowing experiences after being shot were already known. He had been taken to 47 Parker Street and had overheard Merk say, "We'd better hide the kid behind the secret panel." Left alone briefly, he had dragged himself to the telephone and called his mother.

"Good thing you did that," Mr. Hardy said. Then he turned to the policeman at his side. "Mac, would you take Lenny to the hopital? Then drop our prisoner off at headquarters and explain the details to the chief so he can call off his hunt for the boys."

"Sure, Mr. Hardy."

Mac and his colleague carried Lenny outside, then led Mike Batton to the police car. The next instant they roared off.

Mr. Hardy turned to the nurse. "Martha, do me a favor. Drive my car over to our house and tell Laura and Gertrude we're okay. Take Chet with you, too."

"Boy! Will I be glad to get home!" Chet exclaimed. "I'm so hungry I could eat three meals at once!"

"Are you staying here?" Miss Johnson asked Mr. Hardy.

"Yes. The boys and I still have a job to do and we may not get back for several hours."

The nurse nodded and departed, leaving only the three Hardys and John Mead in the mansion.

"What are we going to do, Dad?" Joe asked eagerly.

"Follow a hunch. Frank told me before that

he'd like to stay and do some special investigating." He turned to his older son. "Okay, Frank. Let's get started."

Frank led the way to the paneled wall in the secret room, pushed aside the bird's wing, and showed his father the three slits which formed the strange Y symbol.

"We tried to find out what to do with them, but had no success," he explained. "Can you tell us anything about this, Mr. Mead?"

The man shook his head. He reiterated his former statement of knowing nothing about the secret devices in the elder Mead's home.

"The whole thing is a great mystery to me," he said.

Mr. Hardy was staring at the unusual ring on Mead's finger. He asked the man to take it off so that he could examine it. Mr. Mead watched eagerly as the detective took a magnifying glass from his pocket and studied the Y symbol.

Suddenly Mr. Hardy smiled and moved something with his fingernail. To the amazement of the onlookers, the three pieces of the Y raised up in the shape of a miniature key.

Quickly the detective inserted it into the slits on the wall and pulled open a small door.

The others gasped. Within the opening beyond lay stacks of money!

"Does—does that belong to my uncle?" Mead asked.

Mr. Hardy quickly checked the serial numbers of the crisp bills. "No. It's new. Judd Merk's haul!"

"From his television thefts?" Frank asked.

"Exactly."

"But where do they sell the stolen sets?"

"I found out they have a large operation on the West Coast. The goods are shipped to a factory there, then taken out of their original cabinets. The thieves replace them with cabinets carrying the brand name *Soli*, which they make themselves, and, with the necessary modifications, export them as their own.

"But why do they use the Mead house to hide the money?" Frank asked.

"It's only temporary. Merk sets up a spot like this in each area where he plans to pull a series of burglaries. Since it is far removed from the actual plant, there is less chance of its being discovered. Also, none of the gang lives here, so it's really quite safe."

Mr. Hardy took a set of ledgers and files out from under the stacks of money. "You see, he used this mansion strictly for the bookkeeping end. If he hadn't tried to make the place into a hospital for his nephew, he might have gotten away with it.

"There was a series of television burglaries in Pennsylvania about six months ago, and the police are sure it was Merk's gang. But they still don't know where he's hiding out!"

"What about his plant at the coast?" Joe inquired.

"It was closed down by police yesterday. The man who was in charge there never saw Merk, didn't know his name, and only spoke to him over the telephone."

"Where do we go from here, Dad?" Frank wanted to know.

"I have a hunch Merk will come back for the money, even though he knows that we're on his trail. There's a good chance he didn't keep the house under constant surveillance and that he didn't see us."

"In other words, the gang might think that Joe, Chet, Martha, Lenny, and I are still safely locked behind the secret panel?" Frank asked.

Mr. Hardy nodded. "There's one way to find out. "Let's hide and wait until dark!"

CHAPTER XX

The Trap

"Suppose Merk doesn't show up?" Frank asked.

"We'll have the police take over after midnight," his father replied. "He's bound to come sooner or later!"

The detective passed around the sandwiches he had brought from home, then the four settled down to wait. Mr. Hardy and John Mead posted themselves in the inner room behind the secret panel, which was then closed. Frank and Joe turned off all the lights and hid behind furniture in the library.

Just after dusk there came a barely perceptible sound from the hall. The boys stiffened. A moment later they saw a man enter, faintly outlined in the glow of a flashlight. He carried a tool kit and a cutting torch.

The man took a drill from the toolbox. After

searching for a spot on the wall next to the secret panel, he began to bore through the wood.

"He's trying to open the safe from this side," Frank thought. "But he won't get very far." He signaled Joe, and the next instant the boys jumped from their hiding place.

As they did, the man put a match to the cutting torch and a blue flame shot out with a deadly hiss.

"Stand where you are," the intruder snarled, "or I'll cut you in two!"

Joe picked up a heavy chair and hurled it across the room. It knocked the man's legs out from under him and he crashed to the floor. Frank leaped on top of him, and after a brief tussle pinned his arms behind his back. Joe shut off the deadly torch.

"Turn the lights on and open the panel," Frank told his brother.

An instant later Mr. Hardy and John Mead stepped from the secret room.

"We've got him at last," Mr. Hardy said grimly. "You're under arrest, Merk!" He informed the prisoner of his constitutional rights.

"Okay, okay. I know them," the man said, flashing looks of hate at the detective and his sons. He gazed at Mead without recognition. "Another dick?" he asked.

Mr. Hardy shook his head. "This is John Mead, the owner of this house."

Merk sneered, "John Mead is dead." Then he

added, "He was a clever old man, but I guessed his secrets."

"You knew my uncle?" the Englishman asked, astonished.

"So he was your uncle, eh? Sure I knew him. Met him on a train once and got myself invited here," the thief bragged.

Merk could not resist the temptation to boast. He said that the elder Mead had told him about his special hobby of concealed locks and hardware, and even mentioned the safe in the secret room.

"He didn't tell me the exact location, but I found it!" he gloated.

During the conversation Merk had been edging toward the doorway. Now he made a dash into the hall. But Frank and Joe collared him in a second.

"We'd better get this guy down to headquarters," Mr. Hardy said. "Frank, let's tie his hands."

Frank produced a length of rope from his pocket and they secured the prisoner's hands behind his back. Then they all drove to Bayport in Merk's car. On the way, Mr. Hardy coaxed Merk into telling more about his setup. Merk scowled at first, but then told his story with a sense of pride.

The scheme for the burglaries and the modification and sale of the equipment had taken years to set up. When he came to Bayport to mastermind the local break-ins, Merk had heard of

Mead's death and remembered the eccentric's house.

"So you decided it would be a good place for you?" Frank asked.

"Couldn't ask for a better one. Mead had shown me the odd ring with the Y, and I knew about the safe. So, after some investigation and help from a locksmith I had a duplicate made!" Merk smirked.

"And the rest was easy, eh, Merk?" Mr. Hardy remarked. "Well, here we are at headquarters. I'm sure Chief Collig will be interested in your story, and details about the rest of your gang, too!"

A few days later the Hardys and Chet assembled in the Hardys' living room, in anticipation of a celebration dinner Aunt Gertrude was preparing. Questions were asked and answers given.

Mr. Hardy and the police had rounded up the other members of Judd Merk's gang. Jeff proved to be the one who had accidentally dropped the list of TV warehouses and stores near Bilks' garage when he had some work done to his car.

John Mead, it turned out, had his tire changed by Bilks' assistant, but since it was so long ago, he refrained from making a complaint.

When Griff was captured he admitted having taken the old dory from the Mead boathouse and selling it to Chet. He thought Merk did not know about the boat.

"His boss was furious when he found out about the sale," Mr. Hardy said.

"Exactly what made the boat so valuable to him?" Joe asked.

"One night Merk had made a trip by boat to the mansion to store away some cash, but noticed a parked car in front. He had therefore locked the loot in the dory's fish box and left. Griff had sold the boat, then retrieved it, and kept it hidden in a garage until he had a chance to bring it back to the boathouse."

"I should have known!" Chet said glumly.

"It was John Mead's car that Merk had seen," Mr. Hardy went on. "John had just arrived in Bayport."

"Didn't Merk get suspicious that the Mead place might have another visitor?" Joe asked.

"No. He thought it was just a young couple parking away from the road. Obviously this had happened before."

"Well, what about my dory?" Chet exclaimed. "I want my money back!"

"Eh—yes, Chet," Mr. Hardy said somberly, "the police want to talk to you about that. Buying stolen property, you know—"

The doorbell rang. "I believe an officer may be here for that very reason right now," the detective concluded.

Chet turned pale. "B-but I didn't know the boat was stolen. I—"

"Please answer the bell, Chet."

Confused and a little worried, Chet walked to the door. Officer Riley stood outside.

"Just the person I want to see!" he said. "Suppose you tell me everything you know about the stolen dory."

Chet led the officer into the living room and tried, but the words stuck in his throat. In the midst of his efforts, Riley solemnly pulled an envelope from his pocket and gave it to the youth. When Chet opened it with shaking fingers, he gasped:

"Why—it's my money!"

"Right. That guy Griff handed it over," Riley explained. "Just sign this receipt for our records."

"I don't have to go to jail?" Chet asked.

His reaction brought whoops of laughter from Frank and Joe. The little trick they had played on Chet had been worked out beforehand with their father and Riley. For a moment Chet looked blank, then he caught on.

"You win, fellows," he said with a grin.

After Riley had left, Chet turned to Mr. Hardy. "There are still a few questions I'd like answered."

"What's bothering you?"

"Did the same man who stole the records from your files kidnap Martha Johnson?"

"Yes. It was Jeff, the picklock we saw at the county fair. We got his prints as well as some others, but by the time the police received an FBI report, we were already hot on Merk's trail."

Frank took up the story. "Actually, Merk had given Mike Batton the job of finding a way into our house to steal Dad's file, because Jeff was out of town. Batton took a wax impression of our back-door lock. Then Jeff returned sooner than expected and Merk sent him over in case there was a lock on the files. It was the night that Martha Johnson was here. When Jeff overheard that she was a nurse, he kidnapped her to take care of Lenny."

"As far as Batton is concerned," Joe explained, "he was a fairly new member of the gang. He was up to his neck in financial trouble, and a lot of people were threatening him for money. So he did some stealing on the side, cash and jewelry. When we caught him, he was about to hide the gems in the fireplace until he could get rid of them."

"He told me he knew a man named Jack, who would buy them, but it turned out he was lying," Mr. Hardy added.

"Did Merk know of Batton's sideline?" Chet inquired.

"No. Batton was the security leak in Merk's organization. He put us on the gang's trail."

At that point Chet gave a sigh. "Security leak or not, how about some food?"

Frank laughed. "We'll probably have nothing to do from now on but eat. Not a mystery in sight!"

"I wouldn't depend on that," said Aunt Gertrude, who had just entered the room. "As soon as your convertible which Griff wrecked is repaired, you'll be off on something new."

She was right. They would be asked to take on another case even before Judd Merk was brought to trial. It involved a strange search for *The Phantom Freighter*.

"You know, Chet, we almost caught the thieves twice," Frank told him. "Once when Joe and I were in the Mead house, Merk was there too. Jeff was outside and yelled to his boss, 'We'd better go now!' "

"You might have been caught yourselves," Chet replied dryly.

"Right. The other time was when I heard the groan," Joe explained. "It came from Lenny Stryker, while somebody was opening the panel from inside."

"Whew! Did the crooks know you were there?"

"I'm not sure if they were aware of it then, but eventually they found out we were on to them. Merk didn't remove his loot fast enough, though."

"What about the place on Parker Street?" Chet asked.

"They used that occasionally before you went

over there and we all got tricked by Griff," Frank replied.

"I'm glad you fellows got me out of that pickle," Chet said.

"And I'm thankful you are all safe," Mrs. Hardy spoke up. "I never know from minute to minute—"

The doorbell rang again. Mr. Hardy asked Frank to answer it.

"The caller might be Mr. Mead," he said. "I invited him over. On the other hand, it may be news of another mystery."

"We sure hope so!" Frank and Joe said together.

HARDY BOYS MYSTERY STORIES